FIC   Conrad, Pam
CON   What I did for Roman

11A1906

$12.89

DATE			

What I Did for Roman

PAM CONRAD

What I Did for Roman

Harper & Row, Publishers

Cambridge, Philadelphia, San Francisco, Washington, London, Mexico City, São Paolo, Singapore, Sydney

NEW YORK

With thanks to
Kevin and Frank Polignani and Bill Madden,
and also to Roman Brygider and Ray Charles

What I Did for Roman
Copyright © 1987 by Pam Conrad
All rights reserved. No part of this book may be
used or reproduced in any manner whatsoever without
written permission except in the case of brief quotations
embodied in critical articles and reviews. Printed in
the United States of America. For information address
Harper & Row Junior Books, 10 East 53rd Street,
New York, N.Y. 10022. Published simultaneously in
Canada by Fitzhenry & Whiteside Limited, Toronto.

Library of Congress Cataloging-in-Publication Data
Conrad, Pam.
    What I did for Roman.

    Summary: With her mother away on a honeymoon in
Europe, fifteen-year-old Darcie spends the summer with
her dour uncle and his wife, restaurateurs in a zoo
where Darcie begins a search for the father she has
never known and develops a crush on a mysterious seal
and bird keeper who leads her into a test with death.
    I. Title.
PZ7.C76476Wh 1987   [Fic]   86-45497
ISBN 0-06-021331-0
ISBN 0-06-021332-9 (lib. bdg.)

1 2 3 4 5 6 7 8 9 10
First Edition

for M.H.P.

What I Did for Roman

1

JUNE 21

Dearest Darcie,

I just want you to know how much it meant to have you with me yesterday and today. I know it was difficult for you, but believe me, things will work out. We always work things out, don't we? You, me, and now Ed. It will be fine, honey, I promise. I know it'll be a big change for all of us, but Ed really cares about you and—oh, I didn't want to get into all this again. Enough! Just know that as Ed and I travel across Europe this summer, there won't be a day that I won't think of the way you looked yesterday in your pale-green gown with your bouquet and that look of total uncertainty on your face. If only I could reassure you somehow. I love you, Darcie. I will write whenever I can.

Love,
Mom

It was still light outside, but the heavy venetian blinds were closed over the summer windows, setting the room in a cool darkness and throwing blades of hard sunlight painlessly across my legs. This was the bedroom my aunt had prepared for me. It had a thrift shop smell, and there were cracks in the ceiling like rivers in a map of France. I lay there thinking that, outside, the summer solstice was happening. The earth was at a point of pure stillness, like a swing when you get up as high as it will go, before it begins its descent. The entire earth was still, the night and the day perfectly balanced, and even though it was only the beginning of summer and school had just gotten out, everything would begin to lean toward winter again. I could almost feel my feet drag reluctantly through the dust as the swing swept me to a new time, a new tilt.

There was a hollow ache in my chest, but I held it there with my breath and my thoughts, not allowing myself to cry in this room, this strange room, where my aunt and uncle might hear me. I held my mother's letter on my stomach and felt the scratchy bedspread along the backs of my legs. There was a globe light on the ceiling, white once but now gray and dusty, with a few dead bugs lying inside like dry seedpods. My suitcases were by the door, my books, my bike. Uncle George had reluctantly let me bring my bike, but warned me I would have to keep it in this small bedroom and lift it myself up and down the two flights of steps in the apartment building to take it out. He was not going to make things easy for me. He didn't want me here, but Aunt May had wanted me and had promised my mother that it would work out. When we first made these plans, my mother had told me that Uncle George was a good man, a tender man, if I could only get past his hard shell. I had trouble believing that.

I stared at a lamp on the dresser. Its stem was a woman in a hard, flowing gown, her skirt looking like you could bite it and taste stale sugar. The shade was covered with yellowing plastic, and my pocketbook was next to it, filled with photos, some money, makeup, and my phone book, but I knew I wouldn't call anyone while I was here. Not for two months. I wouldn't call anyone. They would wonder what had happened to me.

I closed my eyes, and without aiming, without thought or reason, I flung the letter across the room like a Frisbee. It fluttered to the floor, and I let the tears run down into my ears and my hair. I should have helped with setting the table and all, but I stayed there till Aunt May called me for dinner.

Aunt May's kitchen was like her in every way except size. She was a large woman, and the kitchen seemed only as wide as her hips. The walls were covered with red gingham-print wallpaper so bright and intense that if I looked at Aunt May's head while she bent over the steamy sink, the walls seemed to pound and vibrate behind her. I looked away.

"I guess your mom and Ed should be landing in England right about now, don't you think?" she asked, spraying clear water over a soapy pot.

"I guess," I answered without any feeling, letting the subject die in the air like a hornet hit with bug spray. I studied the plate in my hand, slowly wiping it. Those plates must have been one of my oldest memories, from when I was little and would visit with my mother—creamy white plates with a shaft of gold wheat in the center and a ring of gold around the edge. The ring was worn and nearly gone. There was a chip like a small bite.

"I like these old plates," I said.

Aunt May laughed. Perspiration drew dark rings under her arms. "Oh, they're good old plates, all right. Came in detergent boxes."

"Detergent boxes?"

"Duz, I think it was. Years ago. If you bought a regular-size box, you'd get a dessert bowl or a small cake plate. Giant size would have dinner plates and serving bowls. Life used to be so simple. Come to think of it, that's how I got my glassware, too."

"But why'd you do that? You could've had dishes from the restaurant free, right? Couldn't you just take what you needed from there?"

Aunt May strained to look over my shoulder, past me into the living room, where Uncle George sat before the television set. "Oh, no," she answered in a whisper. "George won't hear of that. Things for the restaurant stay at the restaurant. Things for the apartment stay in the apartment."

I turned and looked in at Uncle George, sitting there with a glass of amber liquid in his detergent-box glass. He was my mother's older brother, much older. I once heard how, when my mother was born, he was the one who called the taxi and took care of all the arrangements. He had more or less raised her, too. He treated her like a daughter rather than a sister, and I guess to me he was like the grand-father I never had. Watching the evening news, he was frowning.

I had never lived in the same house with a man before, so being around Uncle George was like seeing an unknown species close up. A slug. I wasn't used to having a man around on the chairs, in the hall, at the table. I didn't like what I saw. Whenever Mom and I had visited, there would be two moods. When Uncle George was with us, the conversation would be serious, dull, and words seemd to be weighed carefully. Aunt May and Mom were always cautious with him, checking him out of the corners of their eyes, and humoring him. Then, when he *wasn't* around, things would lighten up. We would laugh easily and happily, even loudly—May could be very loud—and I would watch my mother's cheeks flush and her hands fly as she spoke. It was nice when Uncle George wasn't around.

I watched him now as he pushed his shoes off with his feet, never touching them with his hands, never even taking his eyes off the television set, as if his feet were grotesque little animals with minds of their own. His shoes dropped off with dull thuds, and then, when they were off, he removed his socks the same way, catching the tops of them with his big bulbous toes and sliding them off to drape over his shoes. No, I didn't like having a man in the house.

I wondered if Ed did things like that, if he took his shoes off that way. I suddenly thought of the time I had walked in on Mom and Ed after a late band practice and found them listening to records, just the two of them. Ed was in the rocking chair and Mom was on the floor by his feet. His one foot was bare, and she was unlacing his other sneaker with a dreamy look on her face, lost in the music or something. Right where I was, in Aunt May's kitchen, and without meaning to, I closed my eyes and shook my head wildly, the way I do after I wash my hair.

Aunt May stared at me. "What was that for?" she asked.

"Just an itch," I said, scratching my head. "Guess

I still have some rice in my hair." I grabbed for a handful of knives and forks. "You get these in detergent boxes, too?" I asked.

Soon it was dark. Uncle George was still in his chair, but his shoes were gone. Aunt May had whisked them away somewhere. There was a faint scent of vinegar in the air, and from the living-room window I could see the city skyline lit under a great canopy of starless smog.

The room had a yellow glow of old lampshades, and I wandered past the overstuffed brown chairs to the tall bookcase, looking for a deck of cards or a joke book, something to do. There were tons of *National Geographic*s, souvenirs from long-ago trips, plaques from caverns, pencil holders from famous gravesites, and small weird characters made of coarse wood, seashells, and flat doll eyes.

On the bottom shelf was a large red leather-bound book lying on its side, and something stirred in me—an old memory, the almost-scent of my mother's breath—and I pulled it from its dusty place. It was Aunt May's old family album, and I hadn't looked inside it since I was very young, when my mother, Aunt May, and I had sat around the kitchen table, and they would tell me who everyone was, where the picture was taken, and any other details they could recall.

I snapped on the light over the sofa and sat down

with the album on my lap. "I haven't looked at this in years, Aunt May," I said, opening it to the first page. Aunt May stood in the doorway to the kitchen, loosening her apron and hanging it on a hook on the wall.

She came toward me to see what I had. "Goodness," she sighed. "I haven't been keeping it up these last few years, either. Maybe we'll take some pictures while you're here with us, Darcie. That would be nice. Now that you've grown so."

Aunt May sat down next to me, and I was drawn to her, the sofa sagging beneath her weight. She lifted her eyeglasses from where they hung around her neck and peered over my shoulder at the old photos.

The first pages had photographs of Uncle George and Aunt May when they were newly married. I loved looking at them—Aunt May with her face, which was much the same but thinner and younger, and her dresses, which were long and draped, her funny hats, and Uncle George at the restaurant in his white jacket and his ever-present safari hat. Pictures of boat rides, gatherings, and forgotten events.

"That's the mayor with your uncle," Aunt May said, pointing to a man in a baseball cap. "They were great buddies, your uncle and Tony. Great buddies. When we opened the restaurant at the zoo, there were all kinds of opening celebrations, even a parade. Can you imagine?" Her voice was soft, dreamy. And I faintly remembered being told all this once before.

I peered at the picture. Uncle George was standing in front of the restaurant, umbrella tables behind him, the birdhouse off to his left, and I could see he had a fine, pencil-thin mustache then, very dapper. His teeth were pale and uneven, and I could tell he must have been almost handsome once. Except for his eyes—those terrible eyes. He was blind in one eye and it seemed to stare off somewhere behind me when I looked at him. The eye was paler than his good eye, and I often had the sense that he wasn't even seeing me with his good eye. At times I couldn't tell which was the good eye and which the blind, because neither seemed real. Here his hand was affectionately on the mayor's shoulder. Funny. I had never seen him touch anyone like that before. Not Aunt May. Not my mother. No one.

I looked over at him as Aunt May turned the page. How different his face had grown. His nose was swollen, and little veins like delicate roots now lined his heavy cheeks. He seemed to be sleeping— his eyes closed, his hand wrapped loosely around his empty glass.

"Ah! Look!" said Aunt May. "Here's your mother when she turned sixteen. I remember this was the sweet-sixteen party we gave for her at the restaurant. She was so beautiful that day."

I leaned close to the album and studied the picture. I couldn't remember ever seeing my mother like this.

"How old are *you* now, Darcie?" Aunt May asked.

"Sixteen," I said, sensing some great significance as I looked at my mother's sweet-sixteen party years ago. I hadn't had a sweet-sixteen party. Mom had never mentioned hers.

There were other pictures of that day. I wanted Mom's face to be just like mine, but it wasn't. I wasn't a version of her. I was something different. There she was in a pretty outfit—slim slacks, a silky blouse with soft sleeves and a rounded collar that curved beneath her long, straight hair. She was smiling, young, and she didn't even know about me yet. There was no clue in her life that I would someday be with her. It was hard to believe she had even existed on those terms, without me.

"Who's this?" I asked, pointing to a young man who was sitting next to my teenage mother, smiling at her, with an arm possessively around the back of her chair. Had I been told about him once before? Had I forgotten?

Aunt May was very still. "You know who that is, Darcie. That's Paul."

"Paul?" I asked, looking closer. Should I know a Paul?

"Your father," she said, with a note of impatience in her voice.

Our eyes met, and she looked away. She concentrated on another picture and seemed ready to turn the page. I had no memory of this photo.

"Wait a minute," I said quietly, hunkering closer over the page, unwilling to turn, to leave it now. "What was he like?"

"Darcie," she sighed, with a note of exasperation. "This is something you should talk about with your mother. Not me."

I shuddered, remembering how once my mother had mentioned going to the circus with my father before I was born, and the tender skin around her eyes had puckered and the tip of her nose had gone red. I had bolted from the house and jumped on my bike, pedaling as far and as fast as I could, thinking of anything, anything at all except this man who wasn't there, some man who could turn my mother's face sad and scary. Always it had been that way. Sometimes she would say, "Don't you want to know about your father, Darcie? Don't you want to ask me questions?" But I couldn't stand the look in her eyes, the way her voice would crack, and I would turn my back to her, disappear into my room. Once, when I was much younger, I had even clamped my hands over my ears and hummed until she went away.

Now, in the indifferent safety of Aunt May's living room, a faint curiosity welled up inside me, an unfamiliar hunger. I slipped the picture out of its four little black corner holders. Turning and kneeling on the sofa, I held it close to the light. He was a teenager, too. Whenever I had secretly tried to imagine my father in the past, I had pictured a man with a beard maybe, a man who wore vests and smoked a pipe. I don't know what I thought, but this young man, this boy, was not what I had expected. His cheeks were round and smooth like a child's, his hair was tousled and wild, and his mouth was quirky and mischievous. Mostly I looked for my face on this boy. And now, instead of feeling sad not to see my face on someone, I was uneasy to see the shadow of an expression I knew to be my own. His hair was long and curly, curly like mine, and his hairline followed the curve of mine exactly. And his thumb, on the back of my mother's chair, curved up and back like the tail of a written letter, like my own thumb. It meant versatility. My inheritance.

"Are there more?" I asked Aunt May, searching her eyes and seeing she was uncomfortable.

She scanned the photos. "This is him behind your mother when she blew out the candles." Aunt May's voice was low and reluctant.

"Paul," I repeated almost to myself. In this photo he wasn't smiling, but serious and looking right into the camera. Anyone might have thought he was angry, except for me. I knew he was just serious, because it was the way my face was, too. Unless I was smiling, people would ask what was wrong. There was a certain droop to the lips, and a pensiveness about his brow. My mother was making a wish, everyone was laughing and watching, and this Paul was gazing seriously into the camera. At me, it seemed. But he couldn't have known. He couldn't have seen his sixteen-year-old daughter looking at him through time, as his sixteen-year-old sweetheart blew out her birthday candles, wishing for things, wishing maybe for him. I could barely speak or tear my eyes away from his serious gaze.

"Mom was seventeen when I was born," I whispered.

"About that, I guess," Aunt May said, running her fingers up the side of the binding. "Around seventeen or so. I don't think it was too long after this party that all the commotion began. Her getting pregnant and all." She seemed anxious to turn the page.

"Tell me, Aunt May, what was he like? Were they very much in love? Was he a good person? What happened to him?" There was so much suddenly welling up inside me that I was needing to know, aching to hear. And I was grateful there was no pain in Aunt May's eyes, just a discomfort that didn't spill over on me as my mother's had.

"Oh, Darcie," she sighed, but she began hesitantly. "Your mother met Paul in the city here. He lived downtown." Her face softened as she smiled down at the photos in her lap.

I nearly held my breath in anticipation, as if I was standing by a neglected dam that was suddenly overflowing with rain water and ready to burst.

"That's enough!" Uncle George roared. He had gotten up from his chair, the heavy glass slipping from the arm and rolling across the floor. I couldn't tell if he was shouting at Aunt May or at me, his eyes were so wild and scattered. "That's enough!" he repeated, and his bulk swayed before the sofa. "Put that away!" he ordered, pointing at the album. "Are you crazy?"

I was stunned, and felt myself pressing my body into the sofa as Aunt May closed the album with a loud clap and stood obediently. "Yes, George, yes. I will. Now, don't get worked up. For goodness' sake, it was nothing. Really. Don't."

Vaguely I remembered my mother telling me that sometimes, if Uncle George had too much to drink, or if a topic came up that he didn't like, he was given to fiery rages. That's what she had called them—fiery rages—but she had said it with a tolerant smile on her face, as if she'd just said he favored argyle socks or brown umbrellas.

"Get to bed," Uncle George shouted at no one in particular, but he turned to me alone now on the sofa, pointing a finger at me threateningly. His teeth were clenched and his heavy lips seemed to be struggling awkwardly to get the words out. "Forget him, Denise. I don't want to hear his name in this apartment again. Is that clear?"

I nodded, my whole body trembling.

"Now get to bed!"

I got up from the sofa and nearly ran for my room, closing the door behind me. I pressed my forehead against the door, controlling my breath, waiting. I could hear Aunt May scolding and Uncle George grumbling. I looked down at my hand. I was still holding the photograph of my mother sitting next to this young boy, who was smiling at her. I turned the picture over, and on the back, in Aunt May's round, childlike scrawl it said, "Denise and Paul, Sweet Sixteen."

Denise. That's what Uncle George had called me. My mother's name.

Early-morning pigeons scattered before us as Aunt May and I entered the park together. Uncle George had left ahead of us, and Aunt May hadn't said a single word about the night before. She had changed the subject when I tried to speak to her, and hadn't once slowed down or hesitated since we'd gotten off the subway train, even at red lights, where she wove her way in and around cars and trucks, never looking back to see if I was following. Unused to the traffic and the confusion, I flinched at every beeping horn, and the sound of a screeching tire was like a slap on the side of my head. I wondered if Aunt May was angry at me for getting off to a late start and making us miss our ride into the city with Uncle George in his air-conditioned Cadillac.

She had been very careful to instruct me in exactly what train to catch next time, should I ever be late again, because next time she wouldn't wait for me. She would go with Uncle George and I would have to go in alone. As the train had screamed through the tunnels, its lights flickering and its peculiar stench filling my nostrils and saturating my clothes, I had vowed to myself I would never be late again. I would be waiting each morning at that Cadillac. I would wipe the windshield. Anything but this.

"This is where Venezuela sets up the balloon stand," Aunt May was saying as she pointed to a clearing near the benches, which ran in a continuous line along the path. "You'll relieve him for his lunch break." I jammed my hands into my pockets and glanced nervously at the spot. An old man was sleeping on the bench right across from it. His shoes were beside him and his toes stuck out of his brittle socks. I looked away, holding my breath. "That's the path to the carousel," she said, pointing off through the trees. "You won't have to worry about that station, but you should know where it is. If you take the path the other way, it leads to the pony rides." A police car cruised past slowly on a road above us on the hill. "And that's Murphy," she said.

Aunt May was leading me through the park the way a woman would lead a new housekeeper through her house, pointing out dust, fingerprints, and blinds that needed cleaning. I thought longingly of my mother, my house, my room, the job I usually had in the summer being a mother's helper to Mrs. Caleb, playing on the beach each day. My chest tightened with anger, and I walked faster to catch up with Aunt May. I had to put all that out of my mind; my life would never be the same again now that my mother had married Ed. An oily-looking pigeon watched me from the rim of a metal grate litter can. And I tried not to think of the cardinals and blue jays in my backyard as we stepped around a dirty puddle. Suddenly my lungs filled with the remembered scent of jungle animals as we walked through an underpass and entered the zoo.

The yak, a scraggly old rug draped over a drying rack, stood motionless behind his bars. It looked like the same old yak that had been there when I was little, and it seemed he had hardly moved since then. We whisked past him and entered the center court of the zoo. It was as if we were entering another world, and unexpectedly, childhood memories overwhelmed me; I felt myself lightening up, my troubles turning to heavy seeds in my pockets, and as I walked, my pockets tore and they all leaked away. I was a small child again. A child in a tree-lined zoo.

I stopped before a large empty cage that said HOUSE OF LIONS in hand-lettered gold. There were two caretakers hauling big sides of beef to the doorway of the cage. The lions were nowhere in sight, and I waited with a few other people at the railing, forgetting all about Aunt May. A man lifted his small daughter so her feet could stand on the railing, and she sat back on his shoulder. "Watch," he was saying. "You'll see the lions eat their breakfast any minute." She clapped her hands in excitement and waited. A couple standing next to him stared at the beef, the cage, the workers, without saying a word. Somewhere from inside the House of Lions, there were roars, hungry roars. The little girl clapped her hands over her mouth. "Uh-oh!" she gasped.

Maneuvering the huge chunks of beef into the cage, the men positioned the meat in a long line. The roars continued, but before leaving the empty cage, one man swept out the floor, teasing the small audience, saying, "Now don't leave me in here, Jack! Wait for me now!" The little girl had her fingers woven tightly in her father's hair.

Soon both men were out, the door to the cage was secured, a button was unlocked with a key and pushed, and the metal door in the back of the cage slid up with a hum. Five lions glided from the doorway, their large feet padding silently on the cement, their mouths open to show monstrous teeth as they drooled and rushed for the meat.

I was spellbound by the sight of their strong bodies, thickly covered with warm, golden-colored fur. I watched as they lunged around one another, and with growls and grunts they proceeded to devour the meat, holding it between their forelegs and tearing. The meat ripped like tissue paper. They could tear a man apart as easily. But they were beautiful— ancient and noble somehow, with a mystery in their eyes, and an ageless knowledge in the way their weight lolled easily to the ground, as they leaned on one another, totally self-assured.

The largest and what seemed to be the oldest lion looked at me. Our eyes held. He licked his chops in an elaborate show of pleasure, then closed his eyes very slowly on his secret.

I looked up suddenly. All the people had wandered off and I stood there alone. Aunt May was gone, and I rushed off after her in the direction of the restaurant, its roof and flags brightly visible between the thick trees. I meant to find her right away, I really did, but stopped short in the middle of the slate walkway, overcome with yet another scene before me.

A young man was standing on a cement pedestal in the center of the seal pool, with the sun shining like a halo through his dark curly hair and through the thin fabric of his shirt, and all around him in a pinwheel of light rays. It was the very first time I had ever seen Roman Sandman, and it's impressed on my mind for all my life, like a tattoo that will never rub off.

"Darcie!" Aunt May's voice called from the restaurant.

"I'm coming!" I answered, but I didn't move.

I watched him throw glittering dead fish to the hungry seals. They caught their breakfasts in whiskered mouths and called for more. Their playful barks and grunts filled the air, for more and more, until at last he turned his bucket upside down with a flourish, in a show of apology. And then, as if it were the most natural thing in the world to do—I swear to God—he bent down and kissed an old battered-looking seal right on its nose.

And for the first time in two days I was smiling, from my face to my heart, just all-over smiling.

2

THURSDAY

THURSDAY

Dear Darcie—

England is wonderful. We are bushed from all the sightseeing. Hope all is well with you. Ed and I send you loads of love. Hellos to May and George.

Mom

I sat on the edge of the bed, tying my sneakers through a fog of sleepiness. When they were tied, I stayed bent over, resting my body on my legs, my hands collapsed beside my feet on the rug and my hair covering my face. I was staring at the postcard on the floor, message side up, tomb-of-Tennyson side down. "Wish you were here, dear Darcie," I muttered to myself. Wish you were here. Can't even say that, can you? Why not just say, Glad you're not here?

There was a loud rap on my door. Uncle George.

The two-minute warning. If I wasn't ready when he left, I'd have to take the subway. So far, last week and now this, I'd been ready every morning, ready to sit silently in the back of the Cadillac, before rush hour, before breakfast, before clearing my head, to ride toward the city in the thinnest morning light. Each morning I'd get to watch the sun break from between passing iron girders of the bridge.

I ran my brush quickly through my hair, gathering the unruly curls and fastening them with a clip. A golden flush had begun to appear across my cheekbones and nose, from standing in the sun after lunch, selling Venezuela's balloons. Coming close to the mirror, I ran my fingers lightly over the freckles and the bump on my nose. I stared into my eyes, knowing for the first time in my life that I looked like my father, knowing I was sad and wanting to go home.

I heard the front hallway door to the apartment open, tossed the brush on my bed, and was gone. I followed Aunt May and Uncle George quickly down the steps, our footsteps echoing on the staircase, which wound above us like a seashell. Uncle George's prized Cadillac waited at the curb. He treated his car as if it were a good servant or a beloved pet. Dressed in his white jacket and spotless safari hat and sunglasses, Uncle George circled the car as he did every morning, checking for scratches and dents, opening the door for Aunt May, and then he went around to his side, where he slid into the driver's seat.

Aunt May unlocked the back door for me, and once we were all in, Uncle George ran his all-points test of the electrical system. He started the engine, and then each window rolled down and up, groaning softly, and the radio antenna lengthened with a high squeal. He was Flash Gordon preparing for takeoff. He put on his seat belt and rolled the car slowly away from the curb, as if this car, I thought bitterly, unlike the people in his life, needed to be gently roused.

"Did I tell you I'll be able to take driver's ed next semester?" I asked from the back seat.

"That'll be wonderful," Aunt May said, turning to look at me for the first time that morning. She seemed groggy and old, with a certain tightness to her face that could have passed for endurance.

"Shouldn't drive till you can afford to pay for your own insurance," Uncle George said to no one in particular. He snapped on the radio and played electrical games with his side-view mirror.

I pressed my lips together, but couldn't let it go. "That's why I'm working here this summer, so I can save up and pay my share."

"You're working here this summer so your mother can run off to Europe," he said.

I was really growing to hate him. I felt my eyes narrow as I glared at the back of his head.

"Now, George—" Aunt May began, but she let it lie. That's the way it always was with them.

I stared out the window, and watched the neighborhood glide by—the attached houses, the ancient city sycamore trees with trunks like peeling cement, the rolling sidewalks that gave way to underground roots, and the loose manhole covers that clattered as we drove over them. I suddenly longed for the miniature iris that I knew were blooming now by the side of my house. I could almost taste our mulberries, which fell easily from the branches into my hand, sometimes right into my mouth. I looked down at my hands and lined my two backward-curving thumbs together. I was longing for something—I couldn't say exactly what it was, but it was growing inside me like those underground roots, buckling and distorting everything in its path.

Resigning myself to the silence, I watched the bridge appear before us. From a distance and in the morning haze, it had seemed so delicate and frail, the invention of an ingenious spider gone mad, but up close it was just a mass of girders, gigantic screws, cables, and ageless rust, framed in a motley tapestry of billboards, hung laundry, and elevated trains. I remembered hearing about the Frenchman who had once walked across a tightrope strung be-

tween two skyscrapers at this time of the morning—
early, in the misty light, high above commuters and
workers and city businesses, balancing in a magical
world of sunrise and dizzying heights. I leaned my
head back against the plush seat and watched the
high girders and cables of the bridge fly past above
me, sloping up and down, so high that only seagulls
could reach. I imagined in my mind's eye another
young man with wild curly hair. Was it my young
father? Or that seal keeper? I wasn't sure, but he
teetered across the cables, his arms held out, his
feet secure but slow and careful, one at a time along
the twisted cable. He was coming toward me, he
was smiling, and I closed my eyes and smiled back.

On the roof of the zoo restaurant was the famous
old clock, a frozen menagerie of greenish bronze
bears, lions, giraffes, and elephants, each with an
instrument, marching in a changeless circle around
the clock face, which grinned like an ancient moon.
A chorus of "Old MacDonald" chimed through the
trees and the hills of the park as we pulled up behind the restaurant and came to a stop. The clock
chimed seven, and a mist hesitated over the grass
like a protective mother's hand waiting for just the
right moment to let go.

"Get to the tables first thing, Darcie," Uncle George
ordered, climbing out of the car and waiting to

make sure we locked the doors after us. The slamming doors echoed in the morning stillness, and even though I was still angry at Uncle George, I smiled to myself as an elephant trumpeted in the distance, like a behemoth rooster greeting the day.

Out front, past the birdhouse and the path that led to the monkey house, hundreds of chairs were turned upside down on the patio umbrella tables, left as they were from the night before, when they were overturned and the slate patio was hosed down after a day's worth of traffic and meals. Hundreds of chairs, I thought, maybe thousands, and I began counting them mindlessly as, one by one, I turned them back upright and slid them under the tables. Spiders had connected umbrellas to chair legs during the night, and as I snapped their handiwork, the fine strings settled over my arms and hands. I brushed them away and lost count.

Behind me, Uncle George unlocked the bolt on the door of the restaurant, and he and Aunt May, with her mighty, ham-hock arms, pushed the metal grating away from the wide front entrance of their restaurant.

Other workers began to drift in, nodding, waving, always polite to me, the boss's niece, but no one lingered to talk. They went right to work, and soon the noises of industrial coffeepots and bacon spitting and cartons of cookies and eggs and napkins dropping and being ripped open joined the other sounds of elephants, exotic birds, and the distant sound of the polar bear pounding his body against metal bars in a summer warmth he'd never asked for.

I kept watching the seal pool, waiting and looking for Roman. Aunt May had told me his name. The Seal Keeper, she laughingly called him. The Bird Keeper, the Seal Keeper—Roman Sandman. He'd worked at the zoo for the past three years, and he was a real character, she said. She went on as if she were telling me about Venezuela, the balloon man, or the new panther that had just arrived from Africa. I disguised my interest. I asked how old the carousel was. How often the clock got oiled. And when did Roman usually feed the seals? As the last chair was set right, Roman rounded the corner of the birdhouse with a bucket of fish dangling from each hand. I heard Uncle George's metal clicker click four times and twice from inside the restaurant, which was my signal. It meant: Darcie, report to Uncle George.

Roman threw a leg over the railing of the seal pool. His hair was long and wildly curly, like a character from an old Robin Hood movie, and I could see the wiry muscles in his arms straining as he held the full buckets up away from the reach of the seals. Four clicks and two.

In black hip boots, he waded through the moat to the center island, the water sparkling around him and the seals barking with joy. Four clicks and two.

I heard his laughter and his gentle voice speaking to the seals and barking back to them. Joyful. They clamored about him like schoolchildren. Four clicks and two.

I should have waved. I should have called out to him, but I turned, and with my cheeks burning, I ran into the restaurant to find Uncle George.

Each day of work ended in the small windowless office at the rear of the restaurant in a sort of dizzying celebration of money. The first time I was there, I was amazed at the spectacle before me, but now—after more than a week—I was used to it. Aunt May and Uncle George sat beside each other at a long table, where all the cash registers and pushcart concessions had unloaded their earnings for the day. Money was spread to all edges of the table, some of it overflowing onto the cement floor. I had the urge to lie down in the middle of the pile, just to see what it was like, to stick bills up my sleeves, in my socks, in my hair, behind my ears. The first time. Then I got used to it. They say you can get used to anything, and it wasn't long before I was stacking singles and fives and quarters as if they were gin-rummy cards or play money. It took about an hour or so to get it all in bundles and bank bags, tallied up, and then we'd wait for Sergeant Murphy to escort us to the car, out of the park, and over to the bank's night deposit box.

This night Murphy was late.

And Uncle George was impatient. He jammed his hands in his jacket pockets, saying nothing but pacing and watching out the bolted screen door up the path where the patrol car usually appeared. Even though it was growing dark, he still wore his sunglasses, covering those eyes that looked no-where, and I could hear the clicker snapping faintly in his pocket, muffled in his fist, nothing to call for, no one around.

"Murphy's never been this late before." Aunt May sighed, yawning and straightening her stockings. She rolled them neatly around her ankles and tucked them in. "Maybe something's come up."

"Call the precinct station," Uncle George ordered. "I don't want to hang around here all night."

"I don't want to bother them, George. You know they—"

"He's fifteen minutes late," Uncle George snapped, turning to the table and gathering up the bags and metal boxes. "Forget it. Let's just get out of here. I don't need a police escort. We're just taking this to the bank, for chrissake. Let's just go. Grab a bag. Come on, Darcie, wake up."

Aunt May and I both jumped to help him gather up the money. I had learned to do that—to jump. When Uncle George gave an order, Aunt May would jump, and I had picked it up, a certain eagerness, or really a desperation to please, to be good. I didn't like myself when I felt that happen to me. Was this what it would be like with Ed? Would Ed speak and my mother jump? Would I be expected to?

Aunt May had suddenly become nervous. "Oh, George, I don't think we should. You know what Murphy said. Don't even try to get to the car with all this money, he says. There are too many characters hanging around the park this late. It's not safe."

Uncle George made a grunting noise, and with a satchel of money under each arm, he kicked the screen door open and disappeared into the darkness toward the car.

"Oh dear," Aunt May fussed, but she picked up some money and ran after him. "He has no patience."

"Aunt May! Maybe we should wait. Like Murphy says." The money weighed me down, but I didn't move. I wasn't sure if I should do as Murphy said—was it really so dangerous out there?—or get caught up in the pull of the moment, Uncle George's anger presenting its own kind of danger for me.

"Come on," Aunt May called, not even looking back.

In the distance I could hear a hyena laugh, or cry. I cautiously left the office and stepped out into the night. Heavy miller moths had been throwing themselves at the screen door, and now my skin crawled as I felt them batter against my bare legs and arms. I tried to brush them away and catch up to Aunt May. I ran past the darkened birdhouse, and I pictured the birds with their noisy beaks all tucked under dark, downy wings.

I could see Uncle George bending over the trunk of his car, dropping the satchels in and straightening them out. Just as he turned to take the packages from Aunt May, I saw the shadow of a man appear behind him, as if he had just grown up out of nowhere, like those little sponges in capsules that, once wet, swell into animals, hearts, or flowers. He rose up tall behind the rear fender, growing bigger and bigger as he reached up into the sky and came down hard on Uncle George. I saw the glint of a gun in his fist.

Aunt May's scream pierced the night air like a siren. "Help!" she cried. "Help! George! Police!" over and over. Behind us the birds in the birdhouse began to shriek.

The money bags slipped from my hands, my fingers suddenly losing their strength.

"Help! George! Police!"

Uncle George had not gone down. He was still conscious, and now the man was clinging to his back, and my uncle, with a black trickle of blood appearing over his eye, grappled to swing his arms and turn around, but the man was on his back, with his arms around Uncle George's neck. Uncle George was gagging, swinging, and now Aunt May was hitting the thief over and over with her fists, on his back, his arms, whatever she could reach, whatever was close. The gun was waving all over, all over.

"Help! George! Police!" she kept screaming.

Uncle George's knees were sagging as the thief violently jerked at his neck, and Aunt May kept hitting and screaming. The weakness that had come over me left in a burst of fearful energy. I ran toward them, not knowing what I would do but feeling an urge to join Aunt May, to get this man off Uncle George as quickly as possible. Time seemed to stand still. Everything seemed clearer, strobe-light-bright. Sounds were sharp and distinct, as if I had long cardboard tubes pressed to my ears.

"Help! George! Police!"

But before I reached them, someone ran past me, moving me out of the way and then pushing Aunt May away as well. At first I didn't know who it was. I thought it was another thief, but this man had his arm around the thief's neck and had jumped on top of him. The three of them fell in a heap, Uncle George gagging and choking, the thief grunting and growling, and now I could see, it was Roman pulling the thief off my uncle, and Roman yelling, "That's it now! That's it!" He yanked the man's arm behind his back, twisting it, and pulling him to his feet. The gun fell to the ground.

The thief was kicking back at Roman, delivering painful blows to his legs, but Roman held firm, and at that very instant the area was ablaze with headlights. Murphy had finally arrived. He cranked his siren once, and the thief froze.

"Hold it!" Murphy yelled. He was out of his car in an instant, his gun pointed at Roman and the thief, his gun held in two hands out before him as if it were a nozzle and he was going to hose them all down. He took wide steps, looking around him. "Is it just the one?" he shouted.

"Far as we know," Roman answered. He hadn't let go of the man, and they stood motionless as Murphy approached. Then Murphy kicked the gun back toward the patrol car and yanked the man over to the side of the Cadillac.

"Put your hands on the roof, Louie, and spread your legs. One move I don't like and I'll shoot you." Murphy frisked the man, mumbling all the while, patting his arms, his armpits, down his chest, his legs, his socks. "What's the matter, Louie? Nuthin' better to do tonight? Huh?" He seemed to know the thief and treated him roughly.

"Hey, man! Watch it!" The man spoke for the

first time. "You don't have to break my arms. My probation officer wouldn't like that, you know."

"Save it, asshole. Drop an arm." He slapped a handcuff on the man's wrist. "Now the other." The man was cuffed, his arms behind him. "Now get in the car." With a foot, he shoved the man toward the patrol car, opened the door, and then slammed it, locking Louie inside.

Uncle George was sitting up now, his white safari jacket covered with blood and grass clippings, and his hat in his lap. His glasses were intact, reflecting the police car headlights, two round circles of unnatural light, like his eyes. Aunt May was brushing him off, rubbing his cheeks and cooing to him. Her nose was bleeding, but she didn't seem to know or care. "I told you to wait, George, didn't I? Didn't I?"

"I had a feeling about this," Murphy was saying. "Just when I was going to ride over here, I got a call from the other end of the park, and when I got there, nobody was around." He squatted down next to Uncle George. "You all right?"

Uncle George began to get to his feet. Murphy and Roman each reached out to grab his arms and help him up. "Yeah, I'm fine. Didn't want to hang around. Now look. He hit me over the head with something," he said, rubbing his head.

"A gun," Murphy commented, picking it up out of the dirt, clicking it open and shaking it. "Unloaded."

"Now we have to waste a couple of hours down-town filing a goddamned report?" Uncle George, covered in blood and weak in the knees, still had the energy to be belligerent.

"Nah. I'll just get a statement from you now. Tomorrow we'll take care of it." Murphy shook his head. "I had a feeling. Just had a feeling that some-one was trying to get me to the other side of the park, and sure enough. Louie probably had a friend set this up."

I dug in Aunt May's pocketbook and handed her a few tissues. "Your nose is bleeding, Aunt May," I whispered. She took the tissues from me and seemed surprised to see the bright-red blood soak into them. I looked up to see Roman watching me. Our eyes met. I looked away, but back again, and he smiled. I tried to smile, but I didn't seem to have any control of my face. My cheeks were trembling as much as my knees were.

"Let's go into the office a minute," Murphy was saying. "I'll just get a brief statement and let you get cleaned up before we head over to the bank. May, are you all right?"

She nodded.

"Then let's get this over with. Come on," he said, now gentle and soft, taking Aunt May by the elbow and steering her back toward the lit office. They walked behind Uncle George, now steady on his feet.

Without a word, Roman and I began gathering up the packages of money on the ground and putting them in the trunk. I couldn't stop trembling.

Murphy had turned off the headlights, and except for the trunk light and a small street lantern nearby, we were in darkness.

"You're still shaking," Roman said, placing himself right in front of me and stooping slightly to look into my eyes.

I was embarrassed that he could see, that this was the way he would know me and remember me. "I was so scared," I told him, and then, "Thank you for coming like that. I didn't think there was anybody left around here this late. I thought we'd be the last ones out."

I wasn't just trembling anymore. I was shivering. He reached out and put a hand on each of my shoulders. "Breathe deep," he said. "Go ahead, just close your eyes and breathe deep."

I did as he said, my mind a blank except for my terrible shame. I could feel the muscles in my neck trembling, my head like a doll's head on a spring.

"I was staying late in the birdhouse," he said. "Some jerk threw a firecracker in there last night. I found it this morning, exploded, and the birds were terrified all day. Thought I'd hang around and see if I could catch him if he tried it again. It's a good thing I did."

I was taking deep breaths, my eyes closed. I listened to his soft voice, knowing it well from listening to him talk to the seals. Now he was talking to me. I felt the warm press of his hands on my shoulders as my trembling subsided. He slid his hands up my shoulders and gently cupped my neck. I opened my eyes. He was smiling.

"Better now?"

I nodded. "Weren't you frightened just now to run in there like that?"

"A little, I guess," he answered, "but I didn't really think. I just didn't feel like I had a choice, you know?"

I nodded, remembering how I felt running to help Aunt May. "Yes, I know," I said, and then felt suddenly shy, agreeing with him like that. I needed to change the subject. "I watch you feed the seals," I told him.

"Oh yeah? You like seals?" He dropped his hands, and my skin was suddenly cool where they had been.

I like you, I thought. I nodded again.

"Well, I'll have to let you feed them tomorrow."

"Really? You would?"

"Sure. They get tired of me, and I don't get many volunteers."

He was watching me. His face was dark in the night, but for the whites of his eyes and his teeth, which flashed beneath his full mustache. There was a nice smell about him, maybe like seeds or grain.

Something was beginning to happen. I felt it. A sense of not needing to talk with anything but my eyes. My eyes. His eyes. But what were we saying? I was glad it was dark, because my cheeks were hot, my lips dry.

Then, like a balloon exploding in our faces, a shriek filled the air. "Help! George! Police! Help! George! Police!"

"What?" I froze. Aunt May.

But Roman smiled. His face lit up, and still holding me with his eyes, he began to laugh. "It's Tarzan!" he said. Murphy burst from the office, his gun drawn again, his head turning every which way. "What the hell?"

"It's just Tarzan, Murphy. He learned some new words tonight!"

Roman turned and walked off toward the birdhouse, forgetting me already, his hands in his pockets, his head thrown back. "I don't believe it," he was saying, and laughing. I watched him walk away.

"Goddamn parrot," Murphy muttered, going back into the office. "You'd better get in here, young lady," he said to me, seeing me standing alone in the dark.

Without a word I walked toward the office, suddenly sad that the moment was over, as if I had lost something—that old familiar feeling that I'd lost something so precious, someone so precious. As I opened the screen door, Roman called back to me.

"Hey," he said. "Don't forget. Tomorrow. The seals."

"I won't," I answered.

He opened the door to the birdhouse, and loud cries of "Help! George! Police!" sounded from inside, filling the dark, eerie emptiness of the zoo.

Not many people came to the restaurant the next day. They never did when it rained. And it was just as well, because Uncle George was particularly nasty and Aunt May was as jumpy as I had ever seen her. Her hands trembled, and it seemed no matter what I said to her, she'd answer, "Not now, Darcie. Not now." I made myself scarce.

The tables and chairs were set up, but there wasn't much hope of anyone sitting on the patio in the rain. The umbrellas were for sun, not rain, and the fringes dripped continuous puddles onto the seats. I looked over the wet chairs, wondering how old they were and if two of them could have been the very seats my mother and father had been sitting on in that photograph from my mother's party. They looked the same. I could touch them, and maybe I could touch one and know that this was where my father had once sat. I wanted to find the right two and put them together at the same table.

I sighed sadly, watching the sheets of rain slash past the entranceway to the restaurant. I was leaning on the antique cash register, my arms crossed and my chin on my arms. Mary Dora, the cashier who had worked there since the restaurant first opened, sighed, too. But for her, it was a happy, contented sigh.

"It's beautiful out, isn't it?" she asked.

I looked at Mary Dora closely. I couldn't imagine what it would be like to be so fat. All day she sat at the cash register, "the fastest cashier on the East Coast," everyone called her, with her rolls of fat never moving more than an inch this way or that. Her arms were colossal, each one bigger than my torso, and her fingers were like sausages. On her left hand she wore a wedding ring, and a diamond, and they were so tight that she would never be able to get them off. Her fat fingers nearly hid them completely, folding over the circles of gold and silver. I thought of a cemetery fence I'd seen once that had a tree growing right up alongside it. The bark of the tree had pushed against the black metal fence, pushing and growing between the spikes, and then past the spikes to the other side, where it met and melted together to become one bark. That's what Mary Dora's fingers were like, that old tree, growing right around the rings, until one day the rings would disappear and become a part of her.

"I love a rainy day," she said.

"That's because you don't have to do anything," I said, smiling at her, thinking she must be awfully lazy to be so fat.

"No," she said dreamily. "I just love a rainy day. Look at how pretty that is." She pointed out the door at the rain. "I love the way it looks, the way it sounds, the way it smells."

We each took a deep breath. It smelled like soup of the day to me, with a little elephant thrown in. But she rolled back her eyes and smiled as if it were ambrosia. "Ah, how beautiful."

I was getting dreamy, too. I'd been standing there so long the entwined rose pattern on the cash register was impressed on my forearms. I ran my finger over my skin and, looking out at the rain, played tricks with my eyes, staring first at the seal pond, then at the rain before it, back and forth, changing my focus with the sheets of rain.

"A good day if you're a seal," I said, hearing the seals begin to bark as if at a great distance.

Mary Dora laughed. "That's for certain!" she said. "Listen."

I knew their barks. I knew when it was really them and when it was just someone mimicking them, and I even knew the difference between their playful games and their hungry joyful cries when Roman came. Now I could hear their hunger.

Mary Dora and I continued to gaze out into the light rain. It was bright out, and everything glistened—the slate patio, the leaves, the railings. Suddenly out of it came a shrill whistle, the kind I've seen men make at baseball games when they put two fingers in their mouths and curl their tongues a certain way.

"Whatever is that?" Mary Dora wondered, shifting in her seat. It sounded again.

We waited, and now through the rain I could see Roman standing at the railing of the seal pond with his buckets on the ground beside him. He was wearing a black slicker and facing the restaurant, whistling.

I walked to the door, the warm rain splashing up onto my ankles and legs. I squinted to see him better. He whistled again and, this time, waved, beckoned. "Come on," he called. "Chow time."

Now? He wanted me to come now to feed the seals?

"Roman calling *you*, Darcie?" Mary Dora asked. I nodded.

She laughed. "What a fool he is! In this rain."

My slicker was drying over a chair near the door. I picked it up and slid my arms into it.

"You're not going out, are you?" Mary Dora asked, her laughter gone. "In this rain? Are you crazy?"

"Thought you said it was beautiful, Mary Dora," I said, not looking back at her.

"From here," she answered. "I like it just fine from here."

I snapped my slicker closed up to my chin and secured the hood over my head. I hesitated in the doorway. "If Uncle George comes looking for me, tell him I'll be back in ten minutes."

"You'll be wet all day," Mary Dora warned, but I was gone.

I stepped out into the rainy day, and as if in a wonderland, a fairy tale, I walked deliberately to where Roman stood balanced on the edge of the seal pool.

"Good morning, Roman," I called, feeling a little more brazen today, as if the rain were a veil to protect me, or a tentlike covering that brought us close, I wasn't sure which.

"What's your name?" he asked, handing me a bucket. Rain dripped from the curls around his face and down his nose.

"Darcie McAllister."

"Well, Darcie, you want to feed them from here? Or do you want to go stand in the middle?"

"The middle," I told him.

He climbed over the railing with his bucket and started across the walkway in the moat. He wore hip-high boots, but the water in this part came only to his knees. I hesitated for the slightest moment, and then I took off my sneakers and socks and tucked them beneath the steps. I headed out after him, the water cold and clear about me. The seals escorted us, barking—I swear, nearly smiling—and one jumped behind me, his wet, warm body brushing against my legs.

Roman stopped in the middle on the small concrete island. He smiled at me. "A seal lover, huh?" he said to himself, it seemed. I smiled back, and stood next to him, waiting. I watched how he threw the fish out to the seals, singly, grabbing them by their tails and spinning them out over the seals' heads. I did the same, and we laughed to see the seals awkwardly jump into the air as if their arms were tied to their sides. They seemed good-natured, competing for a thrown fish but forgetting it the moment it was in someone else's mouth. Then they'd look back to Roman and me for the next. Fish after fish, seal after seal. The rain rinsed my face and tasted almost sweet on my lips, and yet the clearest thing to me was Roman next to me, his arm sometimes brushing mine and our hands touching in the bucketsful of dead fish. Once, he even grabbed my finger, thinking it was a fish, or pretending. Later, I would touch my own finger to see if he could possibly have thought it was a fish, or if he had touched me on purpose. "There you go," he'd call out, and, "Thatta boy! Good boy!" He seemed to favor one seal in particular, an old one with sparse whiskers and gray around his mouth.

"Is that your favorite?" I asked.

"Yes," he said, smiling, his face filling with tenderness. "That's Ray Charles. Listen, would you do me a very big favor?" The buckets were empty. His favorite seal grew bold and clambered up the rocks to sit on the cement pedestal beside us.

"Sure," I said. Anything.

"Would you give Ray a kiss?"

The old seal was next to me now, with his nose in my fish bucket.

Roman's face was hard to read. Was he making fun of me? "I always give him a kiss when we're done," he explained. "He kinda looks for it, and well, I think it's good if someone else kisses him now and then, especially a pretty girl, you know, so he doesn't get too attached to me."

Roman's face was serious, almost tender, but his eyes sparkled. I wanted to know more. I wanted to do this again, to be alongside Roman once more. I looked at Ray Charles, old and wizened, who strained up on his flippers next to Roman. Yes. I would do this. I would kiss a seal for Roman.

I bent down for Ray Charles. "Come for a kiss," I called. I heard Roman laugh above me, and felt his hand touch my shoulder. I made smacking noises. Ray Charles looked at me, and in two quick slides was at my side, his gray-whiskered mouth near mine, and we kissed. I could smell fish and wet dog.

"Thank you, Darcie," Roman said. He turned then and led the way out of the seal pool. I followed, with Ray Charles and one of his slippery friends at my heels, and then quickly, without Roman seeing, I ran the back of my rain-wet hand across my mouth. I tasted salt. I shuddered a little inside, but knew it was all worth it when Roman held out his hand to help me over the railing, and he looked at me as tenderly, I thought, as he had looked at Ray Charles. I knew then I'd do just about anything for Roman.

3

TUESDAY

Dear Darcie,

Saw this postcard and thought of you and your zoo job right away. I hope you're enjoying yourself and your stay with May and George. We're having a wonderful time. Amsterdam is especially beautiful, a city of canals, and the people are so friendly. And I'm taking loads of pictures, so when we get back together, we'll have a marathon slide show complete with popcorn, all right? I hope you're okay, Darcie. Love, Mom.

My mother had written in the tiniest handwriting, cramping every word possible into the little message space. The card was from the Amsterdam zoo, and the picture was of the seal pool, complete with fountain of a bronze seal spouting water from his mouth and a smaller seal next to him with a ball balanced on his nose. Beneath the spouting water was a group of playful live seals. They could have been the ones I knew. Could have been Roman's. But next to the pool in the photo, watching intently, was a little girl between her parents, and she was wearing small wooden shoes. I wondered if my mother would bring me wooden shoes. I wondered if my mother had even noticed there was a little girl between her parents, hands held on either side, two hands, two parents.

I sighed and put the card on top of the television set. I hadn't turned on the lights yet, and the living room was beginning to grow dark as I sat there. It was my day off, and after doing laundry for Aunt May and making myself a giant salad for my solitary dinner, I had taken my bike out and ridden all over town. Now, sitting alone in the dusk, an empty plate before me on the low table, I grew restless with my own company. I thought of calling Janie, my friend at home, but remembered she'd probably gone off to her camp counselor job by now. I thought of Betty, Paula, Lainie. But I didn't move from my seat. I didn't want to talk to them. I didn't want them to ask me about the wedding, my job, my stay here. Especially I didn't want to talk to Paula. She was adopted and we'd spent so many hours together imagining what our real parents—in my case, my real father—were like. She was the only one I had ever talked to about my father.

We had made up wild stories and then narrowed

our lineage down to her father, a visiting diplomat from Africa, black as sharp and flat keys on a piano, who'd fallen in love with a beautiful dancer from the Harlem ballet. She'd been the color of light coffee and died shortly after Paula was born, and her father, overcome with grief and fearing Paula was too light-skinned to be accepted in Africa, had flown back to his country in unbearable grief.

Paula liked that. I'd made up most of it, and most of mine, too. I figured my father was a college professor, and my mother had fallen in love with him during her course on American literature. He'd read aloud to the class, given her A's on all her papers, and then they met for coffee to discuss the final and fell in love. I could never come up with a good reason why he left. Actually, it wasn't even a good solution, considering my mother was seventeen when I was born and hadn't even taken any college courses until I was old enough to take care of myself at night while she was at class. It was all wrong, but it was a comfort, just like Paula's story was a comfort. It felt okay, and yet it was open-ended.

Now I thought of telling Paula I had seen a photo of my father and he wasn't a college professor at all. He was a teenager. He looked the way I do when I'm serious. He had smiled at my mother. His thumbs curved gently backward.

I stood up suddenly and walked to the window.

Lights were coming on in the city, or was it the setting sun reflecting on the distant windows? Aunt May and Uncle George would be counting their money now. In a little while Sergeant Murphy would come. Roman would be locking up the birdhouse. Mary Dora had already lifted herself from her specially reinforced chair and slowly made her way to the bus stop. Roman had fed the seals without me. I wondered if he thought about me. I looked down at the card in my hand, Dutch seals. I would show him tomorrow. Maybe tell him about me, a little; ask him about himself, a little.

Unexpectedly, a small flock of Canada geese soared across my view, their profiles crisp and sharp against a deepening lavender-gray sky. Their faint honks filled the air, and an old man passing by on the sidewalk stopped and looked up at them. I held my breath, willing the moment to last. But soon the geese were out of sight, lost in the trees, and the old man faded down the block. I was crying. Maybe I should have tried to call Paula then, to talk to somebody, but I didn't. Instead, I turned and went to Aunt May's bookcase.

My arms already felt the weight of the album as I would slip it out and carry it to my room, but it was gone. There was an empty spot on the bottom shelf where it had once been, just as there was a sudden emptiness in me now that I had seen my father. I ran my fingers over the shelf. I looked around the room, on the table, the chair, thinking maybe someone had been looking through it and had left it out. I knew better, though, deep inside. Uncle George had removed it. Eliminated it. I felt so angry I could feel a faint headache gathering behind my eyes.

I went down the hall to my room. I lay down on the bed and reached my hand up under the pillow where the photo was, the only one I had. I didn't look at it. I didn't have to. I just touched it. And I fell into a light sleep, thinking of sweet-sixteen parties and an unknown young man who had been my father, and then Roman and Ray Charles, and wild Canada geese flying over a concrete-and-steel city where polar bears dream of ice and northern lights.

I don't know how much time had passed, but when I woke, it was dark out and Aunt May had turned on my lamp with the sugar-gown woman and was standing by the bed.

"You all right, dear?" she asked, cupping her hand over my forehead. I could smell cooking smells, cigarettes, and the city.

I stretched and smiled at her. I felt better. Rested. "Yeah, I'm fine." Stretching caught my attention—my knee ached. "Look at this," I said, pulling my knee up and admiring it. I hadn't had a scab on my knee in years. This scrape was huge, and I imagined its scab would be like the bottom of a burned bran muffin.

"How did you do that?" Aunt May gasped, sitting down on the bed next to me.

"Fell off my bike. Hit a pothole." I touched it, but she slapped my hand away gently.

"Don't touch it," she ordered. "Did you wash it?"

"Yes, Aunt May," I answered with a kind of mock obedience.

"Roman was in the restaurant, asking for you today," she said out of nowhere.

"Yeah?"

"Yeah. It seems there's some writer from the Sunday *Mirror* writing an article about the birdhouse at the zoo, and he thought you might like to get your picture taken with the birds for it." She smoothed the bedspread with her hands.

"Oh, I missed it?" My chance to do something besides feed the seals with Roman?

"No. The photographer will be coming sometime this week or next, so just make sure you see Roman tomorrow and he'll tell you when." Aunt May stood and walked to the window. She stared out at the night and then cranked the blinds shut. "Oh, and Roman says to tell you, when you have your picture taken, make sure you wear your blue shirt."

"My blue shirt?"

"Mmm. Roman says to wear the blue shirt, the one that matches your eyes." She looked at me. "Do you know which one he's talking about?"

I nodded and looked away.

Roman knew the color of my eyes. He liked my blue shirt. He wanted me in a picture with his birds.

"Such an unusual man, Roman, isn't he?" she asked, not really waiting for an answer. "Well, it was nice of him to think of you." She ran a hand over my dresser and turned to leave.

Suddenly I remembered something. "Aunt May?"

"Mmm?" Her eyes were tired, circled in dark rings, like smog around the moon.

"That old album. It's not in the bookcase anymore."

"No?"

"No. It's gone. I can't find it anywhere."

"I'll look for it," she answered. "Later." She turned in the doorway, drifting out, away from me, just as I had drifted away from my mother so many times when even the slightest hint of my father had hung in the air.

But that wouldn't stop me now. "Aunt May?"

"Yes?"

"Why didn't my mother marry my father?"

She turned to look at me, and then hesitated, leaning against the doorjamb and slipping her shoes off where she stood. The impression of her shoes remained, the swollen skin still puffed like fresh bread across her instep.

"Darcie, that's something you should talk to your mother about."

"I never wanted to know before," I told her truthfully. "I want to know now. There's a lot I want to know."

"Well, you should have thought of all these questions when your mother was here. You've waited sixteen years to ask, you can wait another few weeks till she gets back." She was as tight and as impenetrable as a clam.

"Can you tell me just one thing?"

"What?"

"What was his last name?"

I held my breath. Would she tell me?

"Your mother must have told you that, Darcie, I'm sure she did. It's Brigadier, Paul Brigadier."

"Brigadier," I repeated. I was sure I had never heard that name before. Almost sure. "What a nice name . . . Paul Brigadier." Darcie Brigadier, I said inside.

"Yes, I thought so, too," she said. "Your uncle used to call him the Pirate." She waved her hand across her face as if a fly had crossed her vision. "I need some coffee," she muttered, and left me there alone.

I could hear the television in the living room,

smell the coffee perking in the kitchen, see the lacy shadow cast on the dresser by the lamp woman's stiff skirt. And now I could taste mulberries, for an instant I thought I could. Brigadier, I repeated to myself, and with my finger I wrote it across the bedspread in round, careful letters. Paul Brigadier.

In the morning I was downstairs and outside before Uncle George had even gotten out of the bathroom. I had carried my bike down the two flights of steps, intending to bring it to work with me so that on my breaks I could ride through the park and get away from those clicks. I was restless, needing a way to get away and be on my own a little, probably the way wild geese feel just before they rise up over a lake and vanish. I was hoping that Uncle George wouldn't refuse me, because I knew he wouldn't wait for me. He'd just leave me there to put the bike back upstairs myself, and then I'd have to get to the city on my own, on the subway.

I stood the bike near the trunk and waited restlessly at the curb, kicking my sneakers against cracked cement and watching up and down the block. It came to me how once when I was really little and not allowed in the street, my mother and I had come to visit Aunt May on a summer day a lot like this one and workmen had been laying a new road. First they would spread gravel across the entire street, and then they would pour black tar over it and flatten it with giant rollers. I had stayed in the walkway to Aunt May's apartment building and watched. Aunt May kept coming down to check on me. She was nervous I'd go in the street and fall under one of the rollers, or maybe get a truckload of gravel dumped on my head. And there was one other thing she was worried about, too—"Don't put any of that gravel up your nose now, Darcie," she warned me.

Aunt May had disappeared into the apartment, leaving me there, and somehow her warning words had created an unbreakable attraction between one of those tiny pieces of gray stone and my nose. Not stepping out into the street, but reaching my hand over the edge of the curb, I grasped a piece of gray stone in my hand, in my fingers, in my fist. I studied it. Now why had Aunt May said that? Why shouldn't I put a piece of gravel up my nose?

I held the piece of gravel on my open palm and held it to my face; yes, my nose. I smelled it gingerly. Nothing. No smell. I held it closer to my nose, let it ease into my nostril like a peanut into an elephant's trunk, and sniffed hard. The gravel was sucked up into my nose, lost. And wouldn't come out. I sniffed and blew, and when tiny drops of blood appeared on my open palm, I flew inside to Aunt May. Not my mother, but Aunt May, who had already known about putting gravel up your nose.

Later, as I sat on the kitchen counter with a towel around my neck to catch the blood, my mother had looked down at the piece of gravel in her own hand and had asked, "Whatever made you do such a thing, Darcie? The things you come up with!"

I smiled now to think of it. It was the beginning of a certain kind of daring for me. If someone said not to do something, I wanted to know why. And when I got a why, I always wanted to test it. And always there's been that moment, that single no-man's-land moment, between wanting to understand why and then, bam, like gravel up my nose, knowing why, fully and completely, with every inch of my body.

Uncle George and Aunt May emerged from the apartment house to find me waiting near the Cadillac with my bike.

"Darcie," Aunt May said, "I thought you were still upstairs! I thought you were going to be late!"

"No, I got down early. I was hoping to put my bike in the trunk."

Uncle George snorted and unlocked the door for Aunt May.

"I know it'll fit, Uncle George," I said, trying to sound as if I wasn't pleading.

"You've got work to do at the restaurant," he said. "This isn't playtime. Or haven't you noticed?"

I gritted my teeth. Where was the patient Uncle George my mother had remembered so fondly from her childhood? The one who had let her stand behind him and comb his hair for hours as they drove each summer all the way to the Catskills?

I spoke nicely to him. "It would be such a help to have my bike with me. I'll be able to get out to Venezuela quicker, if he needs change or balloons, and when Bits needs change over by the carousel, well, I can just zip right over."

Uncle George paused at the trunk. I had hit on his soft spot. Anything for the restaurant. Anything for efficiency. "I'm not lugging it back and forth every day," he said.

"Oh, I know that. I figured I can leave it locked up in the office. You know, behind the freezers. It won't be in the way or anything."

He fiddled with the keys in his hand. I didn't like this feeling that I was having to be sweet and good to get what I wanted. I never had to do this with my mother. With her it was either yes or no. It was as though she never wanted to say no to me, as if yes was always just on the tip of her tongue. Now I waited for Uncle George to grant me a favor. I thought suddenly of Ed, his car, and the books he had already unloaded at my house, and wondered if I'd have to ask him for things or if I'd be able to keep requests private between my mother and myself. I shifted my weight and looked down the street.

Uncle George pulled a key from his ring and unlocked the trunk, which flew open like the mouth of a whale. "That might be useful," he said, softening a little. "We'll try it. See how it works." He lifted my bike into the air and laid it gently in the trunk. It fit easily, with the wheel angled up slightly. When the top closed, I breathed a sigh of relief, knowing it had worked and I wouldn't have to ride the subway this morning.

I hopped into the car behind Aunt May. I felt exhilarated. As Uncle George ran his tests and pulled away from the curb, I settled back in the plush seat and smiled.

"Did you hear about the Sunday *Mirror* and about Darcie going to be in some of the pictures?" Aunt May asked Uncle George suddenly.

"No," he answered. "What's that about?"

"Roman Sandman asked her to be in the pictures. There's going to be an article all about the zoo, and she's going to be photographed with the birds. In her blue shirt, Roman says. To match her eyes!" Aunt May laughed and turned to look back at me.

I wished she hadn't said it like that. And I wished I hadn't looked up at the rearview mirror at that second. I had the distinct feeling that, behind those dark glasses, Uncle George's eyes met mine.

"I don't trust that Sandman," he said ominously.

"Something about him I just don't care for. Don't get too friendly, you hear, Darcie?"

"Mmm," I answered without answering. I looked out the window at the schoolyard and the empty swings and watched them vanish; then the deli, the houses, the parkway overpasses. I bit the inside of my lip and rubbed my thumbs against each other, not daring to look up at the mirror again. I was getting a strange kind of feeling, a stick-some-gravel-up-my-nose kind of feeling. And there was a certain strength to be found in it.

Things were busy in the restaurant all morning and through lunchtime. It was a beautiful, sparkling, sunny day, hot but with a cool breeze that would kick up once in a while. Uncle George kept me running constantly, either working behind the counter dishing out salad and Jell-O or cleaning up tables for the next wave of lunch people.

When there was a lull around two-thirty and he told me to take my break, I went into the office, unlocked my bike from behind the old freezers, and vanished out the back door. I went looking for Roman, to ask about the news article and the picture-taking. The seals had the usual crowd gathered around them, watching their antics and enjoying the cooling water, but Roman wasn't there. He wasn't in the birdhouse, either, when I rode my bike up to the door and peered into its deep, tropical world. I didn't see him anywhere, and decided to just bike off across the park to hear the wind blow across my ears. I wove in and out of the visitors and children, avoiding balloons and cotton candy. The brick path led out of the zoo to the open expanse of hills and trails in the park. I passed the giraffes, their necks dwarfed by the skyscrapers that shot up behind them, and the shiny hippopotamus, sleeping in a pool of mud.

Just before leaving the zoo, I spotted Roman moving quickly through the crowd, his hands in the pockets of his dark-blue work overalls and his curly hair swirling around his head. Before I could call to him, he disappeared into the monkey house, and at the doorway I got off my bike and rolled it inside next to me. I started to call to Roman, but then I realized he was deep in conversation . . . with a gorilla.

"How'r'ya doin', Rebecca?" Roman was saying.

The people who were in the monkey house turned to hear this talk, and one by one they drifted over. Rebecca seemed to recognize Roman. She left her shelf to come sit close to the bars. Her belly was round and obviously pregnant, its skin stretched thin and taut. When she wound her long brown fingers around a bar and looked directly at Roman, he leaned over the railing and touched her fingers gently. He smiled at her, his teeth a white flash that made my heart tighten like a fist in my chest. She bared her teeth back at him.

"Want a smoke, sweetheart?" he asked.

The monkey keeper called out from behind the baboons. "Now, not too much, Roman. You know a pregnant lady shouldn't smoke."

"This is her first smoke all week, Todd. It can't hurt." He turned to Rebecca and spoke intimately, as if they were the only ones around. "Right, sweetheart? How would he know? He doesn't understand what it's like to be in this cage all day long, having to entertain all these people. Yes, yes," he cooed. "You could use a little something to calm your nerves."

Talking to Rebecca all the while, Roman pulled a fat cigar out of his pocket and bit off the tip. He wet it between his lips, twirling it till the tip was dark and moist, and then he reached into his pocket for a light. As he did, he looked up and saw me.

"Darcie," he said, as if he had expected me all along. "Come on over. Join us for an afternoon smoke. I'm sure Rebecca would enjoy some female companionship." He waved me over to his side, and Rebecca reached her hand out to him and snapped her long, dark fingers.

"Patience, Rebecca, patience." Roman flicked a match and held its flame to the tip of the long, fat cigar. More people were gathering around. He inhaled and puffed on the cigar until its tip glowed orange. Rebecca made a gasping noise and banged her hand on the bars.

"There now," Roman said, admiring the cigar, its length, its carefully bitten tip, its glowing ember. He took some exaggerated puffs and held it out to me. "Your turn, Darcie," he said.

I laughed and shook my head. "That's okay. I don't smoke."

"Oh, come on," he insisted. "You'll hurt Rebecca's feelings." He took my hand and pressed the cigar between my fingers. Everyone was watching me, even Rebecca, her yellowed, sensitive eyes waiting. Roman winked. "For me," he said quietly.

Not taking my eyes off him, I lifted the cigar to my lips. For Roman. It was wet. I sucked on the tip, the awful smoke filling my mouth. I wouldn't breathe it in, but just puffed and puffed, the smoke rising around my cheeks and eyes. Roman nodded approvingly. Rebecca moaned now and held out both hands through the bars.

Taking the cigar from my fingers, Roman took another puff and then handed the cigar over to the gorilla, who immediately took it expertly between her fingers and held its tip to her monkey lips. Everyone laughed as she took a deep drag and settled back on her haunches.

"Ah, Rebecca," Roman sighed, "you're one classy dame."

Rebecca threw back her head, and as elegantly as if she were sitting on a bar stool in a red-sequined dress, she exhaled a stream of pale smoke through her nostrils. I'd never seen anything like it. But then Roman put his hand over mine on my bike handle. Some of the people applauded Rebecca, and as she clapped back and took more drags, Roman eased himself out of the crowd, his hand guiding my bike carefully behind him.

Once outside and away from the crowd, Roman led me to a park bench shaded by a large oak tree that made him seem all dappled and dark. He sat down and patted the seat beside him. "You're a good sport, you know that, Darcie?" he said. "Not everybody would do that. I'll bet you love gorillas, too, huh?"

He waited for an answer. Should I tell him it was him more than the animals that I liked? I decided not to. "Yeah, she's quite a gorilla, that Rebecca."

He stretched his long legs before him, his hands in his pockets, his face relaxed and easy. I sat beside him. "Your aunt tell you about the pictures for the newspaper article?" He looked at me, and again I felt as if he were studying me, my hair, my eyes, my chin, taking me all in.

"Yes, she did. I was looking for you to find out when all this is supposed to happen."

"Next Wednesday, so don't forget. Be here." He tapped his finger on my knee. "And have your blue shirt handy."

I felt shy all of a sudden. I was afraid he was going to say something embarrassing about my eyes, or about the shirt I had on now. But he didn't. He just sat there quiet, relaxed in a way I had never known before, a strong masculine peacefulness that seemed to glow from somewhere inside him and cover me like light. It was comfortable just sitting next to him, saying nothing. Watching children. Watching balloons. Pigeons.

Then I remembered the card in my back pocket. "Oh, I wanted to show you something." I pulled it out, unfolded it, and handed it over to him. "Look what my mother sent me."

He held it in two hands and I watched him. His hands were finely shaped, and I had the most peculiar sensation that I wanted to taste them. His skin was smooth and tanned, and the tendons on the back of his hands pronounced and sharp. There were some scars on his fingers and the inside of his left wrist—birds, I remember thinking of birds with their quick, powerful beaks. He turned the card over, reading the inscribed description and even my mother's message, as if he had a right to know everything about me. Strangely it felt okay, as if he did have that right.

"Ah," he said. "Some European cousins! I wonder if they speak Dutch." He barked once and I laughed, taking the card back from him and reading the message to see again what he had just learned about me.

"Your parents are in Holland this summer?" he asked.

"My mother and her new husband," I answered. "And not just Holland but all of Europe. The whole place. And for two months. That's why I'm staying with my aunt and uncle."

"You don't sound too happy. Where's your father?"

I didn't expect that, and I glanced at him nervously. He was looking at me, waiting for an answer. I hadn't had the chance to talk to anyone about my father, not since I had found out about him and had actually seen pictures of him.

"I don't know. I've never known my father. I don't think I even knew his name until just recently. Aunt May told me. And I saw pictures of him."

Roman looked down at his sneakers stretched out before him. He seemed thoughtful. Concerned.

"I'm going to find him this summer," I added, surprising myself. "I think we should know each other."

Roman clasped his hands behind his head and took a deep breath. "Oh, I don't know," he mused. "I don't know."

"What do you mean?"

"It doesn't have to be the greatest thing in the world to know your father, you know. It could be terrible. I wish all I knew of my father was just a couple of old photographs." He smiled sadly. "Besides, it could be, I don't know, dangerous to look for him after so many years. Does he even know you exist?"

I stared at him. If my father knew I existed, wouldn't he have come looking for me? And yet how could he not know I exist?

"You don't know, do you?" Roman asked.

"No," I admitted. I stared off into space.

"You know what?" Roman said, taking my hand between two of his. "Sometimes it's better to just let things come to you. And not force it. Not go looking for something you might be sorry you found. If you're supposed to know your father, you'll know him, in time. Without any effort on your part. Without effort." He clamped his eyes shut. "Now, how did that go?"

He was silent a moment, and then he began to speak slowly and deliberately, as if reciting a poem, and as I listened, all park and zoo sounds faded around me, and it was just the two of us, my hand in his. " 'There's a guidance for us,' " he began. His thumb traced a line across the back of my hand. " 'So place yourself in the stream of wisdom that flows into your life, and then, without effort, you are brought to truth and perfect happiness.' Something like that."

We were quiet. "Ralph Waldo Emerson," he explained.

"Where'd you learn that?" I asked. "In college?"

"Nah, never went to college. I read it in the *Daily News*, the Cryptaquote puzzle." He smiled and looked away from me. I thought about what he had just said, though. "You're telling me not to find my father?"

"I'm telling you to let things happen. Maybe let him find you."

"He may not even know I exist."

"Then if he's meant to know, he'll discover you, just the way you discovered him."

I pulled my hand from his. "No," I said, standing and grabbing my bike, kicking back the kickstand. "That might never happen, and then where would I be?"

"Where are you now?" he asked.

A pigeon landed on the back of the bench where I had just been sitting. Where was I now? I looked into Roman's eyes, and there was such an awful mixture of pain and pleasure in being held in his gaze that I couldn't bring myself to leave him.

"Do you know?" he asked. "Do you know where you are?"

"No," I whispered, my throat growing tight.

"Well, you were just here next to me, and now there's a pigeon where you were." A smile broke across his face, like sunlight across a lake. I laughed at myself.

"Uncle George is probably wondering where I am, too," I said. "Running around with his little clicker."

Roman imitated the clicker. My signal—four clicks and two. Four clicks and two.

"How did you know?" I asked, surprised.

He raised his two hands, palms up, and shrugged. "Came to me in a dream," he answered. "Something I was meant to know."

Blushing, I mounted my bike and pedaled away, but circled back. He was watching me. "I'll see you," I said. "See you around."

"Yeah," he said, holding up one hand. "And don't forget next Wednesday."

Forget? I was counting the days.

Uncle George sent me out to Venezuela in the late afternoon to deliver a last pack of franks and some singles. On my way back, as I was passing the birdhouse, I saw some people drifting out, and I was drawn to it—drawn to the door, to the birds, to the thought of Roman in there, watering the towering trees, laying out trays of seed, whistling. I had thought of him all afternoon, my mind like a rubber ball bouncing off a paddle—one minute I was up, my mind overflowing with thoughts of Roman, the sight of his face, his flashing smile beneath his mustache, the touch of his hand on mine, and the next minute I was down, empty and aching for a father I wanted to find. "Let things happen," Roman had cautioned. I wondered if he was right.

Without thinking, I wheeled my bike over to the doors and steered it carefully through the double entryway, allowing no birds to escape into the real trees, the real sky. Inside, blending with the twitterings and shrieks of birds, I heard the wail of a small child. He was standing with his hands reaching up over his head toward the ceiling. His mother was trying to comfort him, but he continued to stand there with his overall suspenders hanging forlornly around his knees, and his mouth open, wailing, gasping, and pointing up at a yellow helium balloon that must have escaped from his sticky fingers and drifted up to the high, pale-green-glassed ceiling of the birdhouse.

Roman appeared out of a cluster of bamboo, a burlap sack in one hand and a tray in the other. He approached them cautiously, the boy and the mother, and the boy stopped crying as Roman bent and spoke to him.

"What's the problem?" Roman asked, his voice soft and comforting.

The boy stared at Roman, his mouth open, his cheeks wet and smeary. "My balloon." The little boy sniffed.

"Is that all?" Roman asked with exaggerated relief. I wondered what he was up to. "Wait right here a minute, okay?" Roman sprinted to the back room and within seconds he was back with a red balloon, which I thought he was going to give to the boy, but he didn't. Instead, he attached a ball of cord to it and positioned himself beneath the lost balloon. Slowly his balloon rose into the air beside the lost one, whose string was dangling helplessly, waiting to be rescued. The cord passed silently through Roman's fingers, and the red balloon rose higher and higher, until at last it was right next to the yellow one.

Roman began making wide circular movements with his arms, and up on the ceiling the long string began to wind around the dangling string of the lost balloon. Slowly and carefully, with exaggerated seriousness and deliberation, Roman began to pull them in, and the two balloons descended together, their strings intertwined. They bumped against each other. The little boy began to clap, and as he did, the yellow balloon broke loose and wafted back up to the ceiling.

"Aw!" the mother sighed, and the little boy crumbled onto the floor and began to cry again. Roman made a lunge for him, wrapped his arm around his shoulder, and whispered something in his ear. The boy nodded, sniffed, and ran the back of his arm across his nose. He stood up once again and watched as Roman turned his attention back to the balloon. All the while I stood silently at the door, like one of Roman's exotic birds watching from the branches.

I liked Roman's legs. I liked Roman's arms, his broad back and his neck, his intense face lifted to the ceiling, the mischief in his eyes, the almost-humor behind every look and word. I wanted to run to him and hug him, to be a child with him, to be very close, so close.

Again Roman circled the string around the dangling one, this time more circles, and more dramatically. Certainly *this* was not "effortless," I thought, remembering our conversation. When the entire dangling string was twisted around the rescuing string, he began to pull them in once more. Lower and lower. One fist over the other. This time the little boy was quiet until Roman finally reached out and grabbed the bottom of the loose string. Roman handed the string to him, and I watched as he wound the string around the boy's little wrist a couple of times.

The mother thanked Roman and led her son away by his other hand. Roman smiled and bent to pick up his bag of seed and the tray that lay at his feet. I didn't think he had seen me, but now he looked over at me and winked.

"You know what, Roman?" I called.

He straightened and waited.

"Sooner or later that balloon would have come down on its own, you know. Why didn't you just let it come to you? I thought we're supposed to let things happen." I didn't want an answer. I just wanted to tease him, or to prove a point, maybe to let him see that my need was as intense as that little boy's.

His face softened in thought, and the burlap bag tapped silently against his leg. "I guess I just let *me* happen," he said.

Yes, I thought. That was it, to let *me* happen, too, along with everything else. A sort of giddy happiness swelled in my chest as I watched Roman turn and walk away to the back room. His legs were long and strong like a ballplayer's, and the red balloon followed behind and slightly above him like a playful ghost.

4

MONDAY

Darcie—

Forgot to tell you about driving through northern Holland and seeing a sailboat glide through a farmer's field! What startling things have you seen lately? I miss you. We send our love.

Mom and Ed

Uncle George took the turn into the park deliberately and painfully slow, driving along a brick road normally reserved for walkers, bikers, and an occasional patrol car. I turned and looked back at where we had been, idly imagining my father, a young man with curly hair wandering along the brick path on his way to a party. A bright haze hung over the path and the lawns, and even in the early-morning coolness I could see the heat that the day promised. We turned down the path to the restaurant, the three of us still and silent. I had grown accustomed to the quiet heaviness in the air with my summer family, especially when Uncle George was around, and I welcomed my times alone with Aunt May, and the times at work, where there were other people, animals, and—most of all—Roman.

As we pulled up behind the restaurant I caught a glimpse of something happening down the path to the birdhouse. There was a small cluster of men, and something very large on the sidewalk. And it looked as if Roman was with them, squatting beside whatever it was. I saw Aunt May strain to see it, too, but neither of us said anything. Once we had parked, Uncle George immediately took off for the restaurant. I lingered a minute while Aunt May gathered up some packages from the front seat.

"I wonder what everybody was doing down there," I said.

"Down where?" she asked, looking up at me, already forgetting what we had both chosen not to speak of only moments ago.

"Down past the birdhouse, those people, that big thing on the path."

She looked off in that direction. "Oh yes, I can't imagine. Who knows what goes on here half the time." She shrugged her shoulders. "Some excitement. Whatever."

"Can I go see? Maybe help?" I asked.

"Sure. See what it's about," she answered, waving

me away, but then she stopped, changed her mind. "But don't stay too long. You know your Uncle George. I'll do the chairs, but make sure you're back when the breakfast crowd starts coming in, you hear me?"

"I hear you, Aunt May." I put my arm around her shoulders and kissed her soft cheek. "I won't be long."

And it *was* Roman. He was all I was really looking for, and all I saw, but as I got closer I noticed what else was happening and I froze. On the sidewalk, at the feet of Roman and three other men, was a polar bear. It looked like Reginald, the eight-hundred-pound bear often heard banging on his bars. His fur was dirty white, yellowed, his feet life-less on the sidewalk. I noticed his long, dark toe-nails, like giant rose thorns.

"Oh, my God," I gasped. The men looked up at me.

"Don't worry," said Stanley, the bear keeper. "He's dead as a doornail."

I went closer. Now I could see his sightless eyes open, running clear fluid, and his tongue hanging heavily from his open mouth. "Is that Reginald? But how did he get out?"

One of the men wiped his sleeve across his drip-ping forehead. "That's Reginald, all right, but he didn't get out. He died in his cage, and now we're taking him over to the administration building so he can be removed before the zoo opens up. *If* we can figure a way to get him over there."

I looked at the three men who were with Roman. There was Stanley, a short, stocky man, who'd been the bear keeper for years, since I was little, anyway; Lorenzo, a maintenance man I'd seen before in the early zoo hours; and a younger boy, maybe my age, scrawny, with bad skin and ratty old work boots. Roman hadn't even looked up at me yet, but seemed very distraught, caressing the bear's deep fur tenderly as if it were still alive. I realized the younger boy's face was trembling with stifled laughter. He was very jumpy, and I saw him glance nervously at me and around at the others. "I don't believe this," he was saying. "I don't believe this."

"That's enough, Gallagher. Let's try it again. We're running out of time." Stanley was reaching under Reginald. They all began fumbling under the bear together, hands buried deep beneath its fur. They struggled and strained until the bear tilted upright, and then I realized that Reginald was on a dolly.

The four men, all grappling awkwardly with the dolly and the eight-hundred-pound bear, tried to roll it along the path. The bear's legs dragged silently along the sidewalk, its body jiggling lifelessly with every crack in the cement. Then one massive, hairy arm fell open over Gallagher's back. I reached for it and, fumbling, tried to fold it across the bear's chest again, but it was very heavy. Gallagher had collapsed in a heap of terrible laughter. "I can't! I can't!" he was screaming. "Oh, I can't!"

The dolly slipped from their hands, and once again the bear collapsed on the sidewalk, the dolly disappearing beneath him.

"Jesus," muttered Stanley. "He's a heavy son-of-a-bitch."

Lorenzo was beginning to pick up on Gallagher's hysterical laughter. Even Stanley, wiping his hands on the front of his shirt and looking off toward the administration building, was smiling and breathing jaggedly. Lorenzo snorted and hooted, holding his sides and pointing at Gallagher, who in his hysteria had clasped his hands between his legs as if he would wet himself. I smiled, too, ready to join in the infectious laughter, when I looked up at Roman. He was as white as the bear's underbelly, with a tinge of green circling his eyes. My smile froze on my lips. Roman didn't even look at me. He was looking at the bear, a terrible pain in his eyes that I couldn't fathom.

I watched Roman take a deep breath, close his eyes, and then turn on his heel and walk away.

"Roman!" Stanley shouted. "Hey, Roman! Don't leave us now!" Tears were streaming down Stanley's cheeks. "We need you!" He could barely catch his breath, he was laughing so hard. But Roman didn't stop or turn back. He kept walking up the path, and I took off after him.

"Roman!" they were shouting, but he was jogging now and he ducked in the back door of the birdhouse. I followed after him and stood in the darkness. My eyes were useless, after the bright sunlight, but I could smell seed and grain, feel the dampness and warmth, and I could hear Roman breathing. I walked to his shadow. He was standing facing the wall, his hands on the white tile and his head hung between his arms. I placed my hand on his shoulder, wanting to comfort him. It was as if he were counting his breaths. Inside, in the main room, I could hear the birds' frantic squawking and singing. I could feel Roman's cold, clammy skin beneath his shirt, and I was silent with him.

Soon he spoke. "Damn it," he whispered. "Every day he'd pound on those bars. That pounding, that terrible pounding. That's what he died of."

I knew what Roman was talking about. I'd often heard Reginald throwing his body against the bars in the distance, its dull thud carrying through the trees. "He was just a bear," I said softly, easing my hand away, suddenly awkward to be touching him. "He didn't know."

But it was as if I weren't there. "I kept wondering if he remembered," Roman went on. "I wondered if he remembered where he came from—ice caves, arctic storms, midnight suns. And if he was missing them."

"Stanley told me once that Reginald was born in Minnesota, Roman," I said. "The zoo bought him from another zoo." I thought it would comfort him, soothe his mind, but he looked at me as if I didn't understand anything.

"I think he remembered," he said simply. Leaning his back against the tiled wall, he slid down to the floor. He stretched his arms out before him, his hands clasped in a tight fist and his head hanging. "Sometimes," he whispered, "sometimes I just can't stand this place. All these cages." He lifted his face to the ceiling and I could see he was crying.

A tiny, brightly colored finch had found its way out of the main birdhouse into the back feed room, where we were. It had been twittering above us all the while, landing on windows, on the light, and now it landed on the floor before the door. Roman stared at it, not seeming to see it at all. Then suddenly he crept to the door on his hands and knees. The bird posed, perfectly still. Roman reached the door and gently pushed it open. Wide. The bird looked around the room in three little jerks, took a small hop, and then disappeared out the door. Gone. Free. And I knew in danger.

"Why'd you do that, Roman? That bird'll die out there." I was suddenly angry at him.

Roman closed the door and stood up, looking at me for the first time. "Yes, but at least it's free now, isn't it?" He slowly picked up the feed bags for the birds and walked to the screen door, the entrance to the main room.

"Oh, Roman," I whispered, feeling disappointment wash over me in a wave. But Roman was gone.

I didn't see Roman the rest of that day. I never caught a glimpse of him feeding the seals the next day, either. I saw one of his helpers in the seal pool during the afternoon, but no Roman. And I didn't go looking for him, because I thought he might be embarrassed. Only once in my life had I seen a man cry—it had been Ed, and as it was with Roman, it left me with a helpless ache, like feeling the supports of a country bridge weakening as I walked across.

I thought about Ed and that afternoon last fall. I had been with him and my mother in Ed's backyard. It was a cool autumnlike day, with a crisp Canadian smell in the air. The memory of that day sticks like popcorn in a back tooth. The more I work to forget it, the deeper it goes.

Ed was barbecuing, and my mother was lying on a lawn chair reading the Sunday papers. Thinking about it now, I guess it was right around the time I realized my mother had begun to love him. I was in Ed's deep canvas hammock in the shade, working the crossword puzzle, and asking for help now and again, sending my voice up out of my canvas cocoon like a puff of smoke when I was stuck.

"Seven-letter word for *reasonable*, starting with *L*."

Mom and Ed would answer, sometimes not, and then after a while I just let the paper drop over my face, surrendering to my sleepiness, the cool breeze, the sway of the hammock, and the smell of chicken rising in the air on sizzling smoke. In a while they forgot I was there.

Then, as if in a dream, I heard Ed begin to talk about his younger brother, who had died years before. I guess he'd never told my mother much about this brother before, because I heard her ask questions and lead him tenderly through a long, rambling account of his childhood. Baseball games, boyhood brawls, nighttime adventures. I half listened. He laughed at his memories, his long-put-aside past, and then said that today was his brother's birthday. They stopped talking, and I could hear the chicken being turned, the rack being raised. Then it was too quiet. I heard my mother's softest voice. "It's okay," she was saying. "It's really okay." She whispered something else to him, too. I don't remember what it was. Something about love and death. I lifted my head out of the deep-slung hammock and saw the two of them standing there, holding each other. I could tell they were holding each other tight, the kind of tight that uses every muscle in your body and leaves you trembling. Ed's face was buried in my mother's hair, and they stood absolutely still. I don't think they were even breathing.

I remember ducking my head back in the hammock, feeling embarrassed and scared. I looked up at the sky, all I could see of it, the long slit of it through the hammock's opening from below my feet to above my head, and I wished for a bird to fly past, or an airplane, anything to escape into, but there was just blue, the empty quiet, and the ache of seeing my mother comfort Ed and hold him like that.

Ed had been comforted, but not Roman. I didn't know how to do the right thing, I guess. The right words, the right touch. I don't know any more about men than I do about giraffes or camels. It's as if it's all a big mystery and somewhere along the line I was expected to pick up some special knowledge and I just never did.

It was a full two days later, the day of the picture-taking, that Roman's path finally crossed mine again. I was so busy with the lunch crowd that I didn't even notice when he first came in. But soon I heard the laughter. I could see them all at a table across the restaurant—Roman, Mr. Sherwood, the zoo director, and Alice Molloy, his assistant, Uncle George, a man with three cameras in front of him on the table, and a beautiful young woman I had never seen before. I had the impression she was about the same age as Roman; I don't know how I knew that, except I suddenly felt as if I were about four years old myself.

Between counting out change and tallying up items on trays, I kept my eyes glued to them. I was surprised after seeing Roman so upset about Reginald to see him smiling now, and although I couldn't hear what he was saying, it was obvious he was making them all laugh, especially the beautiful woman, whose hands were as graceful as a peacock's tail, fluttering first to her throat and then touching the back of Roman's hand on the table. I watched him through her eyes—his noble sort of nose, cut strong like a chisel over his dark mustache. His brilliant eyes, which held like a handshake, and his perfect teeth, his infectious smile. He was wearing a blue-and-white-plaid shirt I had never seen, with his sleeves rolled up to his elbows. I watched her fingers hesitate on the back of his hand and then on the curved muscle of his forearm. I didn't know her, couldn't hear what she said, but *I knew* I would hate her voice and the way she smelled.

I watched her then through his eyes—her presence as smooth as velvet and as rich as a bouquet of exotic flowers. A pale scarf draped perfectly about her elegant neck, and with precise, enameled fingernails she raked her dark, loosely curled hair away from her face. She leaned toward Roman and said something to him, something not meant for the rest of the table, and I swear he strutted; without even getting out of his seat, he strutted like a damned baboon. I hated her.

Four clicks and two. Four clicks and two. Uncle George was watching me through his dark sunglasses. When I looked at him, he signaled for me to join them. I knew I couldn't, I couldn't see Roman now, have him see me, and even as I knew these things, I stepped out from behind the counter and walked toward their table. One of my sneakers was still wet from soup splashing on it earlier in the day. I could hear my toes squishing. I was wearing the blue shirt Roman had asked me to wear, and although I had been pretty sure of myself this morning as I stood in front of the mirror, my eyes bright and my cheeks flushed with excitement, now all I could think of was the inside of my sneaker.

"This is my niece, Darcie McAllister," Uncle George was saying, his arm extended toward me as I approached. His fingers encircled my wrist like a handcuff and I stood there. I had lost my ability to smile, I was sullen; I didn't dare look at Roman.

"Darcie, you know Roman"—still didn't look at him—"Mr. Sherwood, Alice Molloy, and this is Veronica Lyle and Victor Branowitz, from the *Daily Mirror*. They've come to take pictures and interviews today for that article." Uncle George was using his business voice, gracious, bigger than life. I wondered where the arrogance went, the meanness. I could feel his fingers burning into my wrist, and without drawing attention to it, I pulled away from him and thrust my hands into my pockets.

"Hi," I said, trying to smile.

This Veronica tapped a cigarette out of a leather case and lit it while I stood there. She leaned back, took a deep draw on it, and smiled at me, unsuspecting, totally oblivious of the image I was superimposing on her—that of Rebecca, in all her gorilla dignity, Rebecca with a pale scarf draped perfectly around her hairy neck, her heavy, thick fingernails painted blood red, toying with a fat wet cigar. Just another one of Roman's women, I thought to myself. My smile widened now, more genuine.

"Roman says you'll be joining us for the bird photos." Veronica was waiting for me to say something.

I said nothing. I felt Uncle George shift uncomfortably in his seat. Out of the corner of my eye, I could see Roman looking at me.

"In a peacock-blue shirt, too," Roman said. He was smiling. I looked at him now, as if he had held his hand out to me, to take my hand. "Tarzan loves to sit on a blue shoulder," he added. It was like a slap.

"Who?" Veronica turned toward him, and her smile for him was different than it was for me. It was as if it held invitations and promises.

"Tarzan, the parrot," he said. Roman was telling them how Tarzan loved the color blue. So Roman had never liked me especially in blue. He didn't care what I wore. I was wearing blue that day for a lousy parrot. And what about the polar bear? Had he forgotten all about it? So soon? Before I had even figured out how to comfort him about it? I felt as if I were in a bubble, watching the table from far away, Roman entertaining and funny, Veronica Lyle alluring and smooth, and everything else a prop for a scene where I didn't belong.

"I gotta get to work," I said, taking a step back. "It was nice."

"Why don't you come over to the birdhouse around three, Darcie?" Roman said. "We should be ready for the pictures by then, don't you think?" he asked, turning to the photographer.

"Right," I muttered, tossing off a loose kind of salute and not waiting for any further instructions. I turned on my heel, hearing the broth squish between my toes as I walked away. "Over my dead body," I muttered. "You can just go kiss a slimy seal—"

*   *   *

At three o'clock Uncle George clicked for me, and when I looked over at him, he pointed to his watch. I just nodded and slipped from behind the counter. I took my apron off and draped it over a chair in the back room. I pulled my bike out from behind the freezer and edged it out the door, leaving the noise and smell of the restaurant behind me. Then I put the birdhouse behind me, the zoo, Roman and his lady friend, and I pedaled as fast as I could in the other direction. The path led over a slight swell and into the heart of the park, acres and acres of rolling hills, benches, trees and boulders of slate rock jutting up out of the earth. I biked farther than I had ever gone before, away from the paths and the people, and I would have biked away from myself as well if I could have, but always I was there, my arms before me, my hands on the handlebars, my legs pumping away, and my head with its face, my Darcie McAllister face, and every once in a while I sobbed.

I didn't know why I was crying. I was just so angry. Angry about working at the zoo this summer, angry that my mother had left, angry that Roman had forgotten Reginald so easily, angry that my nails were short and colorless, angry that I was so young, angry at Roman, dumb, stupid Roman. I pulled my bike over to the shade of a huge tree and threw myself in the grass beneath its branches and cried.

They'd be taking the pictures now. Without me. Without my blue shirt, which Tarzan would have really loved. I pounded the grass with my fist. My mother always told me I cried too long, that a good cry should be like beating pancake batter, that you do it just long enough to mix, but not to get all the lumps out. But I didn't stop, not until my eyes were bloodshot, my voice was hoarse, and my legs were as weak as starfish legs.

Maybe if I'd had a father when I was growing up I would have been different. He would have gathered me onto his lap and made everything better. His sweater would have been scratchy like the grass. He would have taken his pipe out of his pocket so it wouldn't hurt me. And he would have given me a Chiclet or something and said wise words. But that was my professor father, my imaginary father. I couldn't use him anymore. I thought of my real father as my crying eased and I rolled over on my back. His youthful eyes looking out of the photograph at me. In my mind I climbed up into the tree. My father. It would be strange if he'd really gone on to become a professor, with leather patches on the elbows of his jackets, carpet slippers, a basset hound to keep him company. Or maybe he'd become a truck driver, or a TV repairman, or a songwriter, or a hotel manager. Maybe he lived in Florida now, or Alaska, or South America. A long sigh swelled my body and I let it go. I was done crying.

A feeling of total weakness settled on me like dust. All the things I had no control over weighed me down—Roman, my mother, Uncle George, the zoo. But for the moment the thought of my father didn't seem so heavy. Maybe there was still a chance with him. Maybe not everything was lost. After all, wasn't I a Brigadier, too? I knew the old me, the Darcie McAllister me, would have run away forever, but there was a new part of me, barely visible, like a root cracking its way through an acorn, but it was there, the Brigadier part, the part that was ready to know. And I knew I could find him. Especially if he still lived in the city, as Aunt May had mentioned, if he hadn't moved since he knew my mother. Some people live in the same neighborhood forever. I sat up and felt like a patient waking from a coma. Every muscle ached. I was dizzy, weak, but I was done crying. There was something I had to do. And I was ready now.

I raised my bike and slowly mounted it, taking stock of where I was for the first time, trying to orient myself, trying to figure which way it was to the city street, the park exit. I could hear the traffic, see the brick wall in the distance. I had left the zoo far behind. I'd go back later. When the photography session was over. When I had done what needed to be done.

Pedaling off to the street, I sensed a new energy

swelling inside me. There was really some hope, a thin ray of sunshine. I felt my swollen face with my hands and stopped at a stone water fountain to take a drink and splash the metal-tasting water on my cheeks and my eyes. I searched my pockets for change.

The traffic was heavy in the street, rush hour already beginning to build. I pedaled over the wide sidewalk along the edge of the park, looking up and down each block for a phone booth. There was a single booth across the street, but when I maneuvered the bike across, I discovered there was no phone book. I went up the block to the next wide avenue, the park and its trees fading behind me. Another block and another, till finally I came to a bank of phone booths, each bearing a heavy, black-covered phone book, thick and worn. It opened immediately to the B's.

B. B. B. Baily, Benson, Brandon, Breton, Brig, Brig, Brig, Brigadier. Could this be him? Only one. P. Brigadier. 47 VanCouver, KL5–3259. I stood there, not sure what to do next. I could call him and say, "Hi, this is Darcie, your daughter." Or no. I could say, "Hello, are you familiar with a woman named Denise? You went to her sweet-sixteen a few years ago. . . ."

My palms were sweating. Chances were he wouldn't even be home at this hour, in the middle of the afternoon. He'd be working. I pulled a coin from my pocket. I would just let it ring. I would know what to say. Or maybe I wouldn't say anything this time. Maybe I would just listen to his voice and then hang up. The coin fell into the phone and I carefully dialed the number.

One ring. He was sitting at his desk, reaching across his papers for the phone. Paul Brigadier speaking, he'd say, totally unprepared for the most beautiful surprise of this life. Two rings. He was just coming in the door. He'd drop his groceries on the kitchen table, wishing he had someone to eat with tonight, and reach for the phone on the wall. Yes? he'd shout. Three rings. He'd be in the shower. Hear it any second. Four rings. He'd reach for a towel now. Five rings. No one home. Six. The phone rang on and on in the empty apartment. I saw the plants on the window ledge listening to the ring. I saw the dog raise his head and sniff the air. Seven. Eight. Nine. I hung up.

It was hot in the phone booth, and the traffic and noises were giving me a headache. I tore the page out of the phone book, folded it small, and put it in my pocket. It was all right. Everything would be all right. I knew that now. Nothing else was going right, but this would. And knowing that made everything else seem a little less painful. Roman and his reporter friend. Uncle George and his clicker. My mother and her postcards. Soon I'd be with my father. I'd place my thumbs up along his and we'd understand each other perfectly.

I threw my leg over the bike seat and pedaled back to the zoo. I was more daring now, weaving in and out of traffic, back to the trees and the coolness, back to the gorillas and the elephants and the cotton candy. I felt strong inside.

Uncle George was furious with me when I got back to the restaurant. It seemed Roman had sent his helper over to get me when I didn't show up. I don't think he was so angry about me not being in the pictures as he was that I just took off from work for a while without a good reason. He wouldn't talk to me at the restaurant, but I knew I hadn't heard the end of it. I almost didn't care. Nothing pleased him anyway, and I had given up hoping we'd get along this summer.

But I was shaken by Roman when I finally saw him. It was after the dinner crowd and I was turning over the chairs, getting ready to close up. It was dusk, with a sort of unreal brightness to the air. Everyone in the distance seemed like flat shadows, as if they became two-dimensional as night approached.

A silhouette stood at the railing of the seal pool. I could see the back of him, his head, his shoulders, his boots. The rock in my heart softened. He was alone, and before him in the pool the seals slid silently through the water, over and over, repeating their same patterns, never varying. Ray Charles lay on a flat rock, his body soaking up the last of its heat. I kept on turning the chairs, stopping once in a while to look over at Roman. He didn't move. He seemed perfectly at peace, as if he, too, were soaking up the last of whatever the day had to offer.

When the chairs were turned, all but a few to seat the last of the day's customers, I started back inside. Uncle George had gone over to administration, so the mood was easy and happy inside, but as I turned to go in, I heard the whistle—the two-fingers-in-the-mouth, come-feed-the-seals whistle. It was past their feeding time. I turned to look at Roman. He was watching me. I waved and turned away, but he whistled again, and my heart began to pound. When I looked back, he waved me over. I took my time, going down the stairs from the restaurant one by one and up the platform to the seals even slower.

He didn't say a word. I leaned on the railing and pretended to be watching Ray Charles. Roman settled beside me, his arm close to mine, his hands clasped before him as mine were. I moved away.

"Where were you today?" he asked.

"Went for a ride."

"Thought you were going to come for the pictures."

"Changed my mind."

"I see."

"No, you don't," I said. "But it doesn't matter. You don't have to understand."

"Try me."

I looked at him then, which was a mistake, because my eyes must have been full of my jealousy and anger. The moment our eyes met, his face broke into a tremendous smile.

"Look at this," he said. "Your fur's not lying down flat. Your feathers are all ruffled." He ran his hand down my arm. "Why, even your claws are out. And look." He turned me around. "Your tail is tucked between your legs. That's a bad sign. I can tell about these things, you know. Here, let me feel your nose."

He hooked his fingers over my nose and gasped. "I knew it! And you're such a rare species! We can't lose you. Think of the tourist trade we'd lose if you were gone."

I pushed his hand from my face and looked away. My eyes were filling with tears. "Looks like you got over losing Reginald pretty quick."

I immediately regretted it.

"What makes you think I got over Reginald?" he asked. He reached out and took my pinky in his hand. It seemed silly to pull away, so I let him hold it.

"You were so happy and up this afternoon, with your pretty girlfriend. All smiles and jokes. And I could tell she just thought you were the living end."

He took another finger into his hand; now he had two.

"I see." He was quiet a few minutes and then he asked, "How old are you, Darcie?"

"Sixteen."

"I'm twenty-eight."

I looked at him. "Who's asking?"

"I'm old," he said.

"Ancient," I agreed, turning away.

Ray Charles must have heard our voices, Roman's especially. He raised his head, then disappeared silently into the water, barely splashing.

"I'll bet you're still a virgin," Roman said, gathering another of my fingers into his hand.

Now I pulled my hand away. I felt my cheeks grow hot. "What's that got to do with anything?"

"It's got to do with how young you are and how I'm too old for you," he said.

I didn't answer him with my voice, but I knew he was studying the deepening color of my cheeks. "You don't have to be embarrassed if you're a virgin. It's nothing to be ashamed of. In fact, it's kinda nice."

"Maybe I'm embarrassed that I'm *not* a virgin anymore," I said.

Ray Charles lifted his nose out of the water right near us, raised himself enough to turn around, and then effortlessly plunged back into the water. We watched him. Roman took my hand again, all fingers and palm and wrist.

"I am," I admitted, my defiance leaving me like tension from a sail when the wind dies.

"I'm glad," he said, and he grew quiet.

Ray Charles rose again before us as we laughed, relief, joy. "How ya doin', Ray?" Roman called after the seal. Ray plunged and we followed his dark shadow beneath the surface of the water. "What'd you end up doing this afternoon?" Roman asked, his attention back to me. "While I was slaving under hot lights?"

"I looked up my father. In the phone book."

"Uh-oh," he said.

"I'm just letting *me* happen, like you told me, Roman."

"But you're taking someone's fate into your own hands, aren't you? Be careful, Darcie. He's not a balloon. He's a person. You're talking about someone who's been without you for sixteen years. An awful lot can happen in that time."

I said nothing. No one could change my mind. Not even Roman.

"Tell you what," he said. "Just promise me you'll talk to me before you do anything, okay? Don't just run off and jump into something unfamiliar."

When I didn't answer, he took my chin in his hand and made my head nod. "Yes, Roman," he mimicked.

I smiled and turned away. "Do you know where VanCouver is?" I asked.

"Downtown. Is that where he lives?"

"Mmm."

"Not the greatest neighborhood for you to go wandering around in alone," he said. "Promise me something."

"What?"

"If you do go, don't go alone. I'll go with you if you have to go. But just don't do it by yourself."

"You mean it?" I asked, searching his eyes for a tease or a lie, but he was sincere.

"Sure," he said. "What the heck."

The water before us was turning black and murky as the sun dropped lower and lower. I felt safe and happy now, a friend at my side, Roman there to help me find my father. Ray Charles and another seal swam in circles around the pool, around and around, lifting their noses each time they passed us. I was filled with anticipation. The anticipation I thought maybe only a virgin could feel. Forgetting myself there in the beautiful night, with an elephant trumpeting in the distance and the hot-dog carts rolling home, I forgot my shyness, and like a child, like a baby monkey turning a spontaneous somersault, I swelled inside and I said, "I love you, Roman!"

His warm hand around my fingers turned stiff. He no longer followed Ray Charles with his eyes, but stared vacantly into the water. "Don't say that," he whispered.

"Why? Why can't I say that if it's what I feel?"

"Just don't. You say that to someone and it's like putting them in a cage." He pulled his hand away from me. "Just don't say that."

He didn't hold my hand again. And my fingers felt empty, the way it feels when you wear a ring for a long time and then suddenly stop wearing it. My hands missed his touch and I felt confused. I looked at Roman now, his profile cut dimly against the streetlight, and I remembered a caged cougar I had seen once, sitting very still and staring out over the heads of the people, as if he didn't see them there.

Ray Charles and his friend were gone. They had disappeared under the water, or into their caves. I don't know. They just disappeared, and then, without a word, Roman stood up and walked away.

"Sorry about the pictures today," I called after him.

"It's all right," he answered, without turning.

I ran quickly back to the restaurant through the dark shadows. I ran through a spiderweb, the sticky strings clinging to my neck and arms. I thought I felt a spider crawling over my clothes. Uneasy. All night, every time I thought of Roman, I felt so uneasy.

5

Bonjour, mon ami!
    *Paris is the most beautiful city in the world.
On one of our walks we even came across the
eight-hundred-year-old dwelling of Peter Abelard
and Héloïse. Love stories! Love stories! All around
us! The Eiffel Tower is bigger than you think.
Are you remembering your vitamins? I miss you.
Don't grow while I'm gone.*

        L'amour,
        Maman

I taped the picture of the Eiffel Tower to the
refrigerator and took a can of ice-cold soda. Aunt
May had once told me their apartment gets hot
around the middle of July and holds the heat till
October. I believed her now. It was especially awful
in the evening. No one had turned on the fan since
we'd gotten in, and it stood motionless in the window, merely blocking what air there was. I turned

it to high as I passed and the loud, shrill hum of the cicadas was lost in its whirr.

Aunt May placed a bowl of sliced oranges on the coffee table and collapsed onto the sofa, her shoes off, her housedress clinging to her legs. "Turn that fan this way, Darcie honey," she said, "and come have an orange with me."

I aimed the fan at the sofa. I had changed from my work clothes to clean shorts and a T-shirt, and I frowned at my legs, which hadn't seen much of the sun this year. No beach, no pools. Only my arms and my face were tan. My hands were a deep mocha color, and when I placed them on my pale thighs they looked like they belonged to someone else. "Yuck," I said. "Look how pale I am."

Aunt May patted my hands. "You're very pretty, dear. You have lovely skin."

I made a face. Of course I'd look pretty to an old lady like Aunt May.

"This hasn't been such a fun-filled summer for you, has it, Darcie?" Aunt May asked, her hand still on mine.

"Ah, that's okay," I said, turning my hand over to hold hers. My hand was smooth, and her hand was so different, as if it were made of something else, not skin at all but gnarled wood, speckled and rough but warm.

"I guess you'll be glad when your mother's back

and you can go home and see your friends. What is it? Just another three weeks now?"

Was that all? I hadn't thought about it ending. Hadn't thought about leaving Roman, Aunt May, the remaining untied threads to my father. I didn't have that much time left.

"Where's Uncle George?" I asked.

"Hosing down the Cadillac," she answered.

"He's so hard to live with, Aunt May. I don't know how you do it."

Aunt May took an orange slice and didn't say anything.

"I'm sorry. I shouldn't have said that. It's none of my business."

She put an orange slice in my hand. "Don't be silly," she said. "He's hard, yes. But he's a good man."

I shook my head. "I don't see it."

"That's because you didn't know him years ago, as a young man," she said. "He's been through a lot. He's very sensitive."

I smiled. "That's hardly how I'd describe him. Why won't he let me see the pictures, or ask about Paul?"

She shrugged and repeated, "He's sensitive."

"Insensitive," I corrected, but she shook her head.

"You don't know, Darcie. Don't say that. That was a rough time for him. You have no idea what we went through when your mother got pregnant. I thought he'd die."

"Of what?" I asked, shocked.

"Of sorrow," she answered. "You mother came to tell us. She was shaken and scared, but she thought George might understand and help her. Of course he helped her, but he didn't understand. Not when she wouldn't stay with us. She was barely out the door when he took to bed, crying like a baby. I had to do the restaurant for four days by myself. I didn't know if he'd ever come back. It was like he wanted to die." She looked at me as if telling me a secret. "He was so disappointed in your mother. He loved her very much."

I felt an unexpected rage swelling inside me.

"He loved your mother," she went on. "Like she was his own little girl. She just changed completely in his eyes when she went and got herself pregnant. It was never the same after that."

"But her pregnancy was *me!* It didn't work out so terrible. Didn't he see me when I was born and realize that?"

"He wouldn't let you in this apartment."

I stared at her, stunned. She wouldn't even look at me. "What?"

"It wasn't till you were four years old that he finally let your mother come back up here and bring you. I used to go see you, of course, at your mother's little apartment over by the avenue. You were precious. So bright. I took care of you sometimes, too. At your mother's, of course. Couldn't bring you here. But your mother never stopped loving George. She always knew that in time he'd come around. She never held it against him."

"I can't understand that," I said.

"Who can explain love?" she said softly. "They loved each other, that's all, but love's like a double-edged sword and George had it by the blade. So he did what he could, and then he just crossed her out of his life for a while."

"What do you mean 'he did what he could'?"

"With Paul Brigadier and all."

"What do you mean?"

"Arrangements," she answered.

"What arrange—"

"I don't think we should be talking about this," she said abruptly, getting up and removing the dish of half-eaten orange slices from the table. "You shouldn't be hearing this from me, Darcie. Your mother's the one who should tell you. Not me."

"But my mother's not here, and I never needed to know before. Don't I have a right to know?" I asked, following her into the kitchen.

"Of course you do, but not from me," May answered, rinsing the dish, busying herself at the sink.

I reached across her, shut off the water, and turned her to face me. She seemed resigned, unreachable. "I want you to tell me, Aunt May."

"Oh, Darcie, in a few weeks your mother will be home with your new father and—"

"He's not my father!" I yelled. "I'm sixteen years old! I'm nearly a woman! I have only one father, and God knows what Uncle George did to keep *him* away. Does Paul Brigadier even know I exist? Or did Uncle George wipe us out of everybody's life?"

"Oh, no, no, Darcie. Don't say that." Aunt May eased past me, to reach for a towel, to get out of the kitchen. I followed her. She sat in Uncle George's chair, as if for strength.

"Well?" I pressed.

"Well what?" She was anxious now, her neck flushed, her hair damp and stringy around her forehead.

"Did my father know about me?"

"Sure. Of course he did."

"How do you know?"

"He saw you once. A while after you were born. I thought it was only fair." She was looking down at her hands and then up at me. Her eyes narrowed. "Don't you ever tell George I told you this, Darcie, you hear me?"

"I promise," I whispered.

"Your mother had a doctor's appointment one

day, and I promised I would take care of you for the afternoon. I'd heard Paul was home on leave—he'd joined the army and just finished basic training—and I called him the day before and told him I'd be minding you in the afternoon, if he wanted to see you."

"And he came?"

"Yes."

"He saw me? Did he like me? What happened?"

Aunt May smiled. "Oh, he loved you, all right. It was hard for him to leave. You know how some boys are so awkward with babies? Well, not Paul. He just picked you right up and held you like he'd been doing it for years."

My skin turned to gooseflesh, almost as if I could feel long-ago hands touching me, lifting me. "How old was I?"

"Just a few weeks. I took you to the park. In your carriage. It was a beautiful day. Sunny. Cool. I remember you were wearing a little yellow knitted hat."

"What did he say?"

"Well, he asked how your mother was—"

"No, I mean to me. Did he say anything to me?"

"You were only three weeks old, Darcie!"

"But did he say anything to me?"

Aunt May thought. She folded her hands together. "As I remember, he said you were beautiful, and you smiled." She looked at me to see if that was what I wanted.

My eyes were filling with tears. "Did he say he'd be back for me? That we'd meet again sometime?"

"Yes," she said slowly. "I seem to remember he did. Something about you two would have to have a long talk sometime. Yes, that's it. Said he'd meet you and take you out for a beer one day." She laughed.

"But he never did, Aunt May," I whispered. "He never did."

"You just have to forget about that now, Darcie," she said. "Things don't always work out the way we'd like."

We sat looking at each other. I felt there was more Aunt May wanted to say, and more I wanted to ask, but her face seemed to be collapsing before my eyes. Her eyes wrinkled, her lips pulled in, and her cheeks were dry and old.

"I'm so sad," I said in the softest voice.

She held out her arms to me and I knelt by the chair, my head in her lap, this time not crying but holding it in, all but the tears that soaked into her housedress. I wanted to find him. I wanted to ask him why he'd never come for me. Aunt May rubbed my head and smoothed my hair, until we heard Uncle George's step on the stairway. I got up and went to the bathroom, where I splashed cold water on my face, over and over until my cheeks were numb.

"It's irresponsible!" he was shouting. "This isn't a picnic you're on! You've got a job to do and you do it, just like everyone else on the payroll. Is that clear? No exceptions. Being my niece doesn't give you any privileges."

Uncle George reached into the cabinet and brought down his bottle again. He slammed a heavy glass on the counter and poured some more dark Scotch into it. "I don't know what you think this is, Darcie. You come here, you don't do a goddamned thing unless I tell you exactly—"

"Now, George," Aunt May began softly. "That's not so. You know Darcie has been a great help at the restaurant and around here. I don't know what I'd do without her."

He scowled at Aunt May and brushed past her. "She spends more time off on her bike—"

"Only her breaks, George, you know that—"

"And more time with the goddamned seals and that loony-tune birdkeeper. Tell me"—he turned to me now and put his finger right to my face— "do you wash your hands after you feed those slimy animals? Huh? Huh?"

I was staring at a spot between his eyes, my arms crossed over my chest. I would not speak. He was in another one of his "fiery rages." I wondered what my mother would have done now? Smiled tolerantly? Patted his shoulder and said, There now, George, calm down? All I wanted was to bolt out the door, to run away. But I didn't want to leave Aunt May alone. I knew she'd get the brunt of it, and it would be all my fault somehow. I'd set off something terrible in Uncle George, and although I couldn't stop it any more than I could stop a local RR train, I could stand there and take it, me—the bastard child, the baby who'd ruined the life of his little sister, whom he'd loved so much.

"And do you wash your hands after your little escapades with Sandman?" he went on. "God knows where you go or what you do on your bike jaunts. Ach, you're just like your mother."

I bit my tongue. I stared out the window. My heart was pounding beneath my ribs; I could hear it in my ears. My arms grew cold and prickly.

"Just like your mother. Sniffing after wild-eyed boys, only you're ahead of the game, you are. You go for older men." At first I didn't know what he was talking about. He staggered to the television and clicked it on. "Oh, and that Sandman's a good one, too, about as crazy as they come. You've got great taste, Darcie. He'll take good care of you. You'll never run out of dead fish. Yes, let Sandman pick up the tab this time. No more sucker George.

I'm through with teenage girls who can't keep their pants up—"

"What?" I shouted. I could have killed him. "What are you talking about? I don't believe this! You're crazy!"

He settled into his chair, a sneer creeping over his face. Now he had me. Now I was doing exactly what he wanted. He set his glass down and picked up the TV schedule for the night. Somewhere in the apartment building a neighbor tapped on a wall or a ceiling. "Keep your voice down, please," he said to me calmly. "You're disturbing the neighbors."

But I had lost it. I looked to Aunt May for help, but her face was down and she was busying herself with being invisible, not there.

"I can't stand it here!" I was getting out. Everything in my body screamed to run. I wouldn't stay. I grabbed my pocketbook.

"Darcie." Aunt May stood and reached out to me, but I pushed her away.

"You are a sick man," I shouted, placing myself between him and the television. "You don't know anything! Nothing at all!"

"Would you move, please," he said sweetly. "You're blocking the television." He sipped his drink and winked at me over the rim of the glass.

I was running. Across the room, out the door,

down the steps, and out of the lobby. I ran until I felt a knifelike pain cut into my side, slowing me down. Bent over and out of breath, I leaned against a telephone pole for a few minutes. It was dark, quiet. I walked along, up unfamiliar tree-lined streets, crying softly and trying to calm myself down.

I passed people sitting on their front stoops, fanning themselves, talking quietly. I passed a delicatessen, with no one around. Inside was a pay phone, and I did a stupid thing. First I dialed my own number at home, hoping my mother was there, that this was all a big mistake and she'd come and get me. It rang and rang on the kitchen wall, endlessly, my mother in Paris, no one at home.

Then I pulled the folded page out of my pocketbook. I had been carrying it around, waiting for the right time. P. Brigadier. My breathing had calmed. My hands were steady. I dropped the coin, dialed the number, and this time it rang only twice.

"Hello?" said a man's voice.

I took a deep breath. "I'd like to speak to Paul Brigadier, please."

"You mean Pete?" he asked.

"Paul Brigadier. I'd like to speak to him please. It's very important. This is Darcie McAllister, and —"

"You've got the wrong number." The man sounded old.

Softly the phone rattled, and the line went dead. "But wait—" I dialed again, but this time it just rang and rang and no one answered. Something wasn't right. I walked some more. Down dark streets, with voices swimming lazily in the heat, babies crying, dogs barking once or twice. At another phone booth I tried again, and again no one answered. I didn't understand. Something wasn't quite right, but I wouldn't let it end here. I walked until it was very late, nowhere to go, and when I returned to the apartment, the lights were all off in the windows. I let myself in and stayed awake most of the night.

The next morning Uncle George was a hulk of stony silence, acting as though I wasn't even there, invisible, but Aunt May was bright and happy, as if nothing had happened. I think she was just relieved to see me back, and to know I was safe. She even made French toast and woke me a few minutes early. And it was Aunt May who made it possible for me to get away later at the restaurant.

I was turning hot dogs at the grill—a demotion, I was sure—the front of my apron stained and greasy, and my hair wet and clinging to my face. A tall fan stood in the corner, moving the hot air around over our heads.

That was when I first heard the screams. I looked out over the grill and serving window to the restaurant room and saw people jumping from their seats and scattering. It's funny how people who aren't used to animals can overreact to some things. There were screams and laughter, and people pointing up at the ceiling. Flashes. Flashes of blue and red and yellow, and I saw the big bird dip over the tables, squawking. Aunt May was at my side, drying her hands, shaking her head.

"Oh no," she sighed. "Not again. That one makes the biggest mess. What other restaurant in the world has to put up with this?"

The bird landed on a table and, like a swimmer in flippers, walked flat-footed around the food, knocking things off, sending everyone running. "Go get Roman," Aunt May said. "Tell him Ike's back here again. And I just hope he gets here before George decides to dig out his safari rifle . . ."

I didn't know if Aunt May was kidding, but I handed her the spatula and tore out of the restaurant with my apron still on. As I ran across the path to the birdhouse, my mind was racing—thinking of Uncle George making accusations the night before about Roman and me, and thinking of the uneasy turmoil I still felt after having told Roman I loved him and then having him turn away from me so abruptly.

Roman was in the back room of the birdhouse, measuring out seed and fruit cuttings with one of his helpers. The moment I saw him, my confusion dove into the recesses of my thoughts, and as always, the very sight of his arms, his legs, and his strong back lulled me and drew me in.

"Roman." I leaned into the doorjamb, holding the door open with my foot. He looked up at me, and I was relieved when he smiled. "It's Ike," I said. "He's in the restaurant again. You'd better come quick."

Roman shook his head and laughed. "Oh, Ike," he said. "When will he learn? Out the door and right to the restaurant. What an escape artist he is!" Roman washed his hands and looked at me hard. "What's the matter with you? You look terrible."

I looked down at my apron and brushed the hair off my damp forehead with the back of my hand. "I'm okay," I said.

"No, it's your eyes," he said, reaching over and touching the skin on my cheek. "Big black circles under each eye. What is this—National Raccoon Week or something?"

I felt shy with Roman so close, embarrassed, as if he could almost read on my face what Uncle George had said about us. "Didn't sleep last night," I answered. "Uncle George's giving me a hard time." I shrugged.

"Well, into the bat cage with you!" he teased. He looped his arm through mine, scooped some apple pieces into his pocket, and led me out the door and back to the restaurant. By the time we got there, almost everyone was standing along the walls, watching Ike sample various dishes, flying from table to table and leaving his signature at each one. Uncle George was stalking the room with a big net, looking quite ridiculous in his safari hat and jacket. Seeing him come close, Ike flew up toward the ceiling with its faded murals of ancient elephants and camels and giraffes.

"Oh, looks like we're just in time," Roman whispered to me. "Rama, King of the Jungle, would have cooked Ike, I'm afraid.

"All right, folks," Roman called loudly, his arms raised before him. "Let's be calm. It's true Ike is one of the last known killer macaws, and he could tear a grown man apart with his powerful beak and eat him in two minutes flat—"

The people watching at the edges laughed. I pressed my fingers to my lips. I could have told him again, right there, that I loved him still.

"—but I will brave it, sacrifice myself if need be to allow you to get back to your lunches. Have no fear." Roman reached over to the wall and snapped off the lights in the restaurant. It immediately felt cooler and quiet, with only the outside sunshine filtering through the wide awning windows. He began to whistle, and then, carefully looking at the switches, turned one light back on, a spotlight that sent a shaft of light down to the center of the restaurant. Roman went and stood in it. Like a ringmaster, a magician. Barely breathing, I watched him.

There was an appreciative sigh from the people in the darkness. I glanced around at their dim faces and realized how much I loved this restaurant, this job, this moment. I looked over at Uncle George. I couldn't tell if he was looking at me through his dark glasses, but as I looked at him, his lips pursed in a grim warning. What would he have said if he had heard Roman and me talking that night at the seal pool? I looked away.

Roman began to sing softly, "I-ike. Oh, I-ike. Look what I've got." He had reached into his pocket and pulled out an apple slice. He whistled. He held it over his head in the air, turning slowly in the center of the restaurant, like a rock star bathed in light. What was happening to me? I had to hold myself still, my arms wrapped around me. "Come se-ee," Roman sang.

Ike flew from one rafter to another, his wings flashing yellow and red in the darkness overhead. There was a loud splat on a table underneath him and the small crowd groaned and laughed. New customers wandered in and paused in the doorway.

Roman began to whistle again, a loud two-note call that Ike imitated. There was more flapping, soaring, and then Ike swooped down and in the spotlight landed on Roman's shoulder. Roman's face lit up and he glanced over at me as if he were proud. "That's a boy," he murmured. "Good boy."

I could see Uncle George across the room, a frown gathering on his face. All of a sudden he threw his net against the wall and stormed out the back door to his office.

"Thank you for your patience, ladies and gentlemen," Roman was saying, bowing deeply, with Ike still on his shoulder. He reached up to transfer Ike to his arm, slowly and gently. "You're safe now and you can get back to your lunches." He clamped one hand over Ike's claws and walked out the door into the daylight.

The whole place broke out in applause, laughter, and whistles. I joined them. I laughed and clapped and whooped with the rest of them, not wanting to watch Roman leave. I didn't want to see him simply walk away toward the birdhouse. In truth, I wanted to believe that, as he hit the sidewalk outside, he and Ike would bound into the air and fly off over the trees. My hero. My superhero, who talks to seals, smokes with gorillas, and flies with scarlet macaws. My heart was nearly ready to burst with it, when I heard his whistle.

He was standing in the sunlight, Ike flapping his wings and going nowhere. Roman was waving for me to come. I shrugged, looking down at my apron, feeling trapped, as if I could flap my wings, too, and go nowhere. "I can't," I whispered, not to him, but to myself. But Aunt May was behind me.

"Go," she said, untying my apron and slipping it off my shoulders. "Go. It's all right, sweetie. Don't worry. Go have some fun."

"But it's lunch hour. We're busy."

Aunt May closed her eyes and pushed me in the direction of the door. "Go. Go."

I looked quickly for Uncle George, but he was nowhere around. I hesitated for an instant, and then I turned and ran after Roman, who stood waiting for me. My heart fluttered in my rafters, yellow, blue, and flashing, and I slipped my arm in his and we walked to the birdhouse.

We were quite a trio, Roman, me, and Ike, with his face like a nutcracker and his tremendous, colorful feathers, which reminded me of a dusty old costume. Everyone looked and pointed. Ike flapped his wings once or twice, but Roman had a good grip on his snakeskin claws, until we entered the double door, and there, with the other birds overhead and in the branches of the enclosed trees, Roman let him go and he disappeared. "Thanks, Ike," Roman called after him. "Thanks for the favor."

"What favor?" I asked.

"This was a scheme Ike and I worked out. I told

him to go over there, so I'd have an excuse to go to the restaurant. You see, everyone thinks I captured a bird, but what I really did was to spring you! Ingenious, don't you think?"

I half believed him, even if it was ridiculous. I always wanted to believe what he said.

"Now I want you to come with me," he said quietly. "Do you have about three eons to spare?"

"Only two," I answered, held in his eyes, holding him in mine.

"Oh, those eyes," he sighed, reaching out. He held my head in his two hands, his thumbs pressed gently to the circles beneath my eyes. "Come, my little raccoon," he said. "I'm going to show you something wonderful."

He called to his helper, saying he'd be back in an hour or so.

"I thought you said three eons," I teased, watching him as we walked out the door.

"Three eons to you and me," he answered, "but to Jerry there, it will appear to be just an hour." He smiled and walked quickly along the path away from the restaurant. We walked side by side, our arms swinging but not touching, my stride matching his, the cool shade kissing my neck and face. I felt free and wild; I was sure I could have flown now if I had tried.

We walked up the path to the outdoor carousel,

following the sound of the pipe-organ music—"Casey would waltz with the strawberry blonde, and the band played on . . ."

Roman sang with it. "Always makes me think of a pretty yellow-haired girl with strawberries in her hair," he said. Funny, but I felt jealous. I didn't want him to think of anybody but me.

"I'd rather you thought of Casey Stengel," I said beneath my breath.

He laughed at me. It wasn't that funny, but he threw his head back and laughed, and then he put his arm around my shoulders and drew me close to his side as we walked. I was surprised and didn't know what to do with my hands, my arm along his body. I hooked my finger in his belt loop and put my other hand in my pocket. The music had stopped.

When we got there, there were only a few small children with their mothers on the carousel. Roman waved to Bits, the carousel keeper, and we hopped up on the revolving platform without a ticket. It was turning slowly, about to start again.

"Pick a steed, Lady Darcie. Whichever one you want. And I'll slay any dragons that stand in your way."

I walked against the revolution, feeling slightly dizzy and uncertain on my feet, walking from brass pole to brass pole, staying even with the tree on the sidewalk but passing horse after horse, all medieval marvels, painted brightly, with trailing scarves and feathers and ornate harnesses and saddles. A beautiful white horse came toward me, with yellow plumes and purple tassels. I swung myself up on it, and it sank beneath me, sank and then rose gently, over and over, as the carousel moved on.

"Wise choice, Lady Darcie," Roman said approvingly. "Rode him myself into battle just last week. Just watch him, though, he's squeamish around birds. He gave Ike a terrible time, and Ike was my second-in-command. It was a disaster."

I never knew quite how to react when Roman went on this way. I'd usually laugh, but now I just smiled and ran my hand over the hard mane of my mount. Roman rode one right behind me, a black horse with its head thrown back and its mouth open to show thick white teeth and a brass bridle. Wild eyes.

I hadn't been on a carousel in years, and this particular one even longer. It was soothing. Calming. I let myself be carried away, drifting up and down, around and around. I didn't even look back at Roman; just knowing he was there was enough. I wanted to ride forever. Here was a fantasy world where no one could reach me, nothing mattered. And within a glimpse, a sigh, was Roman, as close as the brass ring. As the song ended and the carousel slowed, Roman was at my side.

"Follow me," he whispered. "Now I'll show you something wonderful."

He took my hand, and instead of leading me off the platform to the outside, he led me into the center, and there we jumped off onto solid ground. In the center of the carousel was a broad circular column decorated with mirrors and gaudy stripes, and the pipes of the organ were lined up against it. On the side was a door, which Roman opened, and he led me inside. It was dark. The only light was some sun leaking in from above us. He held his finger to his lips. "Shhh. Listen."

There were no sounds, except the distant cry of children clambering on board. Roman's eyes glowed white in the darkness. Suddenly a cranking sound began dully somewhere beneath us, and then, in an explosion of sound, so loud and frightening that I clamped my hands over my ears, the organ music began, resounding full force in the dark tunnel where we stood. I felt Casey waltzing with the strawberry blonde through every hair and fiber of my body. It was coming from everywhere, from all around me, even from the bones inside my own head. Roman's face was lit with excitement. "Ever heard anything like that?" he shouted.

I shook my head. Never. Never before. I wanted to run out the door, but he silently urged me to follow him up the circular staircase, higher and higher, until we were up in the awning, the peak of the carousel, where the flag hung in the still air. There was a thin opening where we could see out, and while the music piped up from below, vibrating through the clothes on my body and into my skin, we looked out over the park, its trees and rolling hills, and off in the distance, the roof of the restaurant.

"Make a wish," he shouted. He was very close to me, our legs touching. And he was looking at me now, the sun a slash across his face like a mask.

I squinted through the slit out into the distance. If I could have anything I wished for. Anything at all. I made my mind a blank, like a dark, cloudy pond, and then like a cork, my wish popped to the surface. Roman had lowered his ear to my lips and was waiting. "I wish I could talk to my father," I shouted. "I would like to go see him."

Roman was silent. All the happiness and foolhardiness was gone from his face. Had he thought I'd wish for something else? Did I see disappointment in his sun-slashed eyes? He studied me. We looked at each other in perfect stillness, surrounded by the deafening music high up in the carousel tower, where wishes are made and promises are sealed.

In time, maybe in two eons, the song came to a close, and the tunnel seemed to collapse with silence, as though the music had been a physical presence there with us. But Roman and I were still looking at each other. And then, as if he had clamped down the visor on his armor and raised his silver shield, he promised. He whispered, "It will be done." And I knew he meant it.

I fed the seals nearly every morning with Roman after that. They learned to wait for my morning break from the restaurant. And I had lunch with Roman almost every afternoon, late in the day on my other break. I knew he believed in letting things come to him, and happen in their own time, so I didn't press him or rush him about going down to VanCouver Street. He had promised me we would, and I believed him. I waited.

It was at the end of a long, hot week, when Mary Dora stepped back into the kitchen before leaving for the day.

"Can I borrow your niece for a few minutes, Mr. McAllister?" she asked.

I was startled. Uncle George was gathering the money from the cash register and supervising the closing of the restaurant for the night. He wouldn't refuse Mary Dora anything. He was the one who had originally called her the fastest cashier on the East coast, and he knew he could count on her to be there at her register every day, and for the count to be accurate every night. He was always especially polite to her.

He acted as if he had barely heard her. "Yeah, sure," he grunted, and then turned away, preoccupied.

Mary Dora winked at me and beckoned me to follow her with her big, sausage-like finger. I threw down the sponges I was using to wipe the chrome counters and went with her. She had a rolling gait that swayed from side to side, and her legs had a funny snap to them, as if her knees worked differently from most. I walked beside her on the wide sidewalk, reminded of the giant balloon floats soaring high above me long ago, at a Thanksgiving Day parade. It wasn't till we were some distance from the restaurant that she spoke to me. She stopped and caught her breath.

"They told me to bring you," she said, panting.

"Who?" I asked.

She smiled at me. "The monkey keepers. They have a surprise for you. This isn't something that happens every day around here. This is your lucky day, girl," she said mysteriously. She continued to shuffle on, her one hand flapping at her side and the other gripping her small pocketbook to her enormous breasts.

"You'll see, you'll see," she said, waving my questions aside and plodding along. She led the way to the monkey house. She let me open the door for her and squeezed sideways through the narrow opening.

Unlike during regular visiting hours, the monkey house was gently lit, the corners dark and secretive, the walls echoing our footsteps. The small monkeys were drowsy shadows on perches, in branches, in corners. A few men in overalls were standing by the last cage, Rebecca's. They were murmuring quietly. As we approached, one raised his finger to his lips to silence us. I tiptoed, still not knowing why.

Mary Dora pushed me ahead of her, to the railing outside Rebecca's cage, and the monkey keeper motioned me to duck under the railing and come close to the bars. He hoisted me up onto the cement ledge and jumped up beside me. "Look," he said quietly, and then I knew.

Rebecca, in a halo of light and warmth, looked up at us placidly. She was lying against the wall on a bed of straw and blankets. And in her arms was the tiniest fuzzy ball, a gorilla baby. They were both very still, and then the baby stirred, a little rear leg stretching, a hand grasping the air, its face turned out to the light and then back into Rebecca's warm fur. It looked so human, so much like a little person. Even Rebecca looked more human than ever before. Her large hairy brown hand took on the gentleness of the most demure lady. She softly cupped her baby's small behind to draw it closer, and with two delicate fingers she touched the baby's head, parting its hair, turning down its tiny ear.

"It's a girl," the keeper whispered, "so you know what we've named it, don't you?"

"What?" I asked, looking at him, seeing a sort of pride I imagined you might see on a father at a nursery-room window in a hospital.

"Darcie," he said, smiling at me. "Darcie, the baby gorilla. They're making up the signs right now. We'll keep the crowds away for a bit, but she'll be a fine attraction, especially since Rebecca's so tame and such an entertainer."

I was hardly paying attention. Darcie. They were naming this tiny gorilla after me. I held on to the bars and watched Rebecca drift off into a contented sleep.

The keeper turned back to Mary Dora. "Wanna come up here, Mary Dora? I'll give you a lift—"

"Not today, Todd." She laughed. "Think I'd pull the bars down on top of me, and then you'd be in trouble. Well, Darcie, what do you think?" She reached over the railing and tugged on my sock.

"It's amazing," I said. "Look how tiny."

"I guess she has gorillas named after her every day," the keeper said to Mary Dora over his shoulder. "No big deal."

"Oh, but it is!" I answered. "It really is! But why me? I'm surprised."

"Well, it's kind of unofficial zoo policy to name

new animal babies after people who work around here, and you're the newest this summer, and seeing you're your uncle's niece and all, and well, Roman mentioned it to me, he thought it would be a good idea. After all, Darcie's a nice kind of unusual name, and see?—she even *looks* like a Darcie, don't you think?"

The baby gorilla raised her little fist twice, knocked on her mother's barrel chest, and continued sleeping. Rebecca looked at me with old, yellowed eyes that held intelligence and secrets. "Yes, she looks like a Darcie," I said. What an unusual world, I was thinking.

A furry little Darcie, born in straw and in darkness, was to be raised in a cage, never to know a jungle, never to feel rain in her eyes, never to speak. My eyes welled with tears. I blinked them back. That was ridiculous. I was beginning to remind myself of Roman. I coughed to clear my throat. I'd have to ask Roman if there was an animal named for him. And I'd ask him if Ray Charles ever worked here. I smiled again. It had been Roman's idea. Name it Darcie if it's a girl, he must have said. He had thought of me.

6

Dear Darcie,
    *All of Rome is like an old museum. I think
I am getting tired, and looking forward to coming
home and starting life. Had a dream you brought
a lion cub home for a pet. We'll have so much to
talk about when we're finally together again.*
                    All my love,
                    Mom

By now I had taken my bike out from behind the freezers at the restaurant and moved it permanently into the back room of the birdhouse, where I could get it whenever I wanted to without Uncle George keeping track of me. I had also gotten my own pair of high rubber boots. They were cold and clammy against my legs, but I never pulled them on that I didn't feel a light happiness in my heart, a wild giddiness in knowing that I was about to wade into the center of a pool filled with hungry seals and make them all love me. Sometimes during the day, if I passed the pool and one of them saw me, he would begin to swim wildly back and forth. It made me smile.

I lifted the bucket of fish and silently followed Roman out of the supply building toward the pool. There were a lot of camp groups at the zoo—clusters of children in identical orange or yellow T-shirts, herded along by patient adults carrying cameras and shopping-bag picnics. Roman was quiet. Sometimes he would be so talkative, looking into my eyes with every word he spoke, brushing my hair back absentmindedly, or shooing a yellow jacket away from my arm. But then, other times, he was so quiet and withdrawn, deep in his own world and thoughts. At those times I thought maybe he didn't want me there. Maybe I was in the way. But he never showed any impatience or annoyance. He just wasn't there, and I became accustomed to waiting.

I followed Roman into the seal pool, watching his body move beneath his shirt and his loose work pants. I saw his face as he bent to put the bucket down; it was serious, almost sad. I couldn't understand how someone so beautiful could not be happy all the time, just happy to be such a celebration of muscles and curly hair and skin. But there, at last, high on the pedestal of rock and sunshine, Roman came to life. He smiled for the first time that day and dug into his bucket. He spun the shimmering fish high into the air over the heads of the seals. His fingers glistened.

Ray Charles rolled his head back and dove into the water. Children at the railing squealed and clapped, and adults pointed to submerged shadows that shot past almost like sharks. I could think of it that way then. Instead of seeing gentle seals, I could alter my mind, like squinting, just by watching them underwater—their dark forms shooting by at frightening speeds, their black fins breaking the surface of the water. In an instant, in a little mind trick, I could lose the joy and put myself in terrible danger. I could do that with Roman, too. One minute he would be the one person in the world I trusted most, and then, as he'd sink into one of his deep silences, it was as if a shadow of a shark had streaked by, and a small quiver of fear would pass through me.

Now he was whistling—"Casey would waltz with the strawberry blonde"—and putting on a show for the children. He had one of the younger seals leaping heavily into the air. Another spun around, another climbed up on the rocks and gave a loud honk that made the children laugh. I threw a fish up onto the rocks for that one and he slithered away. The buckets were empty in no time, and Ray Charles dragged himself up on the rocks beside us and put his nose in the empty buckets, as he did every day. I ran my hand over the top of his smooth head, and he looked up at me with his black, bottomless eyes. Then, without Roman having to coax or ask anymore, I bent over to receive Ray's kiss. He wet my nose and my chin. The children went wild. By now Ray Charles and I sort of expected it of each other. And maybe Ray Charles kissing me, well, maybe that was something he was doing for Roman, too. I didn't mind.

Roman followed me out of the seal pool and I wondered if he was watching me, studying me as I had him. I never saw him do that. Never caught him watching my body, never saw his eyes on anything but my face. Although Uncle George never would have believed that. It wasn't till we were putting our boots and pails away that I tried talking to him and he suddenly seemed to realize I was there.

"Got another postcard fom my mother," I told him, pulling it out of my back pocket. He leaned up against the sink and took it, staring first at the picture of an old cathedral, carefully, as if looking at every window, every gargoyle, every brick; then he turned it over and read the message on the back. "Sounds like your mother misses you."

"Why wouldn't she? She's only been with me for sixteen years, day in and day out. I think it was kind of dumb for her to just take off like this and not expect to miss me." I was trying to sound light and silly about it, but somehow Roman read me like a book.

"You sound angry." He handed the card back to me and crossed his arms over his chest. "Is that why you're looking for your father? To get back at your mother?"

"No," I answered, startled, and then "No," again to myself, inside, asking myself if that could be true. "It's got nothing to do with my mother. I don't know. I've just never been this close to him, or known as much about him as I do now. And besides, there was always something uncomfortable I felt whenever any of this came up with my mother. It's just easier now with her gone."

"Nothing good can come out of an action that's born in anger," he said as if he didn't believe me.

"And what are you now, a guru?"

Roman held his palms toward me and closed his eyes. "When the student is ready, the seal keeper appears."

I glanced down at my mother's card. *We'll have so much to talk about when we're finally together again.* "You know, I *am* angry at my mother," I admitted softly. "Hurt. Hurt, mostly. But that's not why I want to find my father. They're two separate things."

"Tomorrow is your day off, isn't it?" Roman asked.

"Yes," I answered, thinking he was changing the subject and glad of it. "Tuesdays are mine. Why, did you need me for something?"

"Thought I'd take you over to VanCouver Street in the morning and get this out of your system. Thought we'd go early. About eight-thirty or so?"

I stood motionless, the boots in my hand were dripping on my sneakers. He didn't look at me but turned to rinse out the buckets and store them on the shelf. "Do you mean it?" I whispered. "Tomorrow?"

"Meet me at the front gate to the zoo, eight o'clock, and we'll go find your father. I'll take you there." He wiped his hands on a towel and watched me. "You still want to go, don't you?"

"Yes! Yes! I've tried calling, but I only got through once, and an old man hung up on me. He said I had the wrong number, but I don't know . . . there was something about him. I think he knew who I was talking about."

Roman frowned.

"But I want to go there. Yes. But how do I meet you? I don't want to come in with Uncle George and Aunt May. I don't want them to know . . ."

"Take the subway," he said casually, not knowing that subways terrified me.

I was silent, weighing my fears, my doubts. Holding my father in my mind. "Okay," I told him. "Eight o'clock. I'll be here, at the gate."

But Roman must have known. He must have guessed and when I stepped out the front door of Uncle George's apartment house early the next morning, bracing myself for my solo trip into the city, Roman was waiting across the street in the shadows. He raised his hand in greeting, and I was overcome with relief.

"Couldn't sleep thinking about you riding the subway by yourself," he said, coming up alongside me. "I was afraid you'd end up in a train yard somewhere, or in New Jersey."

"Well, I'd be lying if I told you I'm not glad to see you," I said. "I'm nervous enough about maybe seeing my father, and then the thought of the subway . . . but then I knew if I could make it on the subway, I could make it anywhere."

Roman laughed and took my hand in his, as if he did it all the time. And we started off.

"Now the trick is—you have to conjure up the right attitude about this," he said as we pushed through the turnstiles with other people who didn't look at each other or at anything around them. "Think of it as a special place, an underground world of tunnels that connects the whole city to itself, like veins and arteries." The early-morning rush was beginning as we descended into the last level, and the heat pressed around us like a dirty blanket. I could feel it on my arms and my legs, as if I were actually being touched.

"The air's so thick," I said to Roman, feeling panic rising in my throat.

"Look," he said, ignoring me. He was pointing to the wall. There, over a broad advertisement for cigarettes that was covered with graffiti mustaches and obscenities, high above, embedded in the tiles of the wall, was a mosaic pattern. A delicately crafted mosaic of a locomotive speeding through a country scene. It was covered with a grimy silt and barely visible, but beautiful just the same.

"Forgotten," Roman murmured, "and totally unappreciated." Farther down was another mosaic of a flower garden, an arbor. There were more, evenly spaced along the platform, each one more out of place than the next, but untouched by spray paint or vandals, too high for anyone to reach.

"Imagine when these stations were first built," Roman said, "and these wall tiles were being put up. They actually hired craftsmen, probably Europeans, to make these mosaics. They're incredible, aren't they?"

Yes, I told him. I'd never noticed them before. Never looked. I'd just seen the ads, and the scribblings . . .

"They're forgotten," Roman said. "Little pieces of art, covered with grime and nobody ever looks at them anymore. The guy who made them's probably dead. And who even knows? Who looks?"

Roman stood with his hands in his pockets, gazing up at the last mosaic, while a train pulled in behind him. "Promise me something," he said suddenly. He looked into my eyes, serious, intent. "Don't ever come down here without stopping to admire these."

I nodded. "Okay."

"No. I mean it. Even if you have to miss a train, just make sure you admire these every time. So they're not forgotten. And if someone is with you, show them. Tell them about them also, okay? Will you promise me that? Will you do that for me?"

"Sure," I said. "I promise." The train doors were opening and the people around us began crowding in. It was almost as if Roman didn't want to leave the station but just stand there some more, gazing up at the tiles. I got a little nervous and eased toward the waiting train, my fingers tugging lightly on his sleeve. "Roman," I urged, "the train!"

We were the last ones aboard, and as we squeezed in, the doors closed behind us and we were pressed against them, facing each other. Slowly the train slid out of the station. The lights fell away and outside the window was total darkness; here and there a red light whisked by. I cupped my hands over my eyes and peered out. Other tracks glistened beside us, huge girders flew by, black and grimy, everything was dark and filthy, and then we passed through a local station, the lights pale and hopeless, and I saw the people lined up along the edge of the platform waiting for their train, watching us with dead, flat faces. I felt afraid again. An old woman was pressed up against me, and her pocketbook jabbed into my leg with every lurch of the train.

I looked to Roman for reassurance, his face a little above mine in the hard light. We were very close. He smiled. I smiled back, a little.

"Listen," he told me. He pressed his ear against the window in the door. I did the same. The sounds became louder, more penetrating. "Can you hear the drummer?" he asked.

"The drummer?" I listened closely. Closed my eyes. The drummer. Yes, I began to hear it, the wild syncopation, the ragged beat of a mad drummer.

"Can you hear him?" Roman asked.

I nodded.

And his face lit up. "Good," he said. "That's good. Not everyone can hear him. He's something, isn't he?"

Oh yes, I agreed. As the train sped along faster and sometimes slower, the beat would change, from frenzied drumfire to a melancholy throbbing that tore at my heart. I listened and lost myself in my own thoughts of a father who might be waiting for me. Soon we pulled into the station, and the drumming faded away.

Roman led me out the door, guiding me through the crowd and along the station platform. Over the noise of the shuffling, Roman suddenly recited out loud, I guess for me, but others turned and stared at him—"The drummer plays with the stumps of his sticks, and laughs about the books he's burned."

"What's that from?" I asked.

"Would you believe another *Daily News* Cryptaquote?"

"No."

"I didn't think you would," he said, his eyes joking with me again. "Let's go," he ordered, and with my finger latched in his belt loop, I followed him up the steps, out of the depths, and into the sunlight.

I felt as though I were entering a bright alien world. Nothing was real, and my legs were weak and trembling. "Wait, Roman," I said, slowing my step and letting go of his belt loop. "I'm really scared."

He turned to me and then eased us out of the stream of people, where he leaned up against the side of a building and searched my face. "What is it?" he asked.

"I don't know," I said, standing right in front of him. "It's just that the subway makes me feel scared, and then the thought of maybe seeing my father — "

"We can take a bus back," he offered, but I shook my head.

"You don't understand," I said, and tried to find the words to explain. "It's like I *want* to be scared."

He smiled as if he understood and looked up the block, away from me, yet his easiness, the fact that he didn't pry, made me want to tell him more.

I went on. "It reminds me of something, of an old wooden swing when I was little. You know, one of those swings that maybe four people sit on and you face each other on wooden benches?"

He nodded, his eyes gentle.

"There were these five kids who lived across the street from me, all sisters and brothers. It was so weird to me to have that many kids in a family, and then there was me, an only child. I must have seemed like an orphan to them. Anyway, they had this swing, and in the summer, on dying hot afternoons, we'd all pile on this swing that was meant to be gently pumped to make a nice breeze, and we'd pump like wild street urchins till it hit against the wooden roof."

Roman reached out and took my arm, pulling me next to him by the building. An old man in rags stumbled past us, but I went on. Roman's hand stayed resting on my arm.

"We turned that gentle summertime swing into

a daredevil ride like you find in amusement parks. You know what we'd do—we'd take turns. Five of us would pump. We'd put our feet on the seat opposite, two on one side and three on the other, holding on to the handrails with all our might, and get it swinging as high and as wild as we could. We'd have to duck our heads so we wouldn't smack into the roof. We'd watch one another's faces. And the sixth child, the one who was 'it,' would lie on the floor of the swing, holding on to the first slat of wood on the floor as hard as he could.

"I remember when I was 'it.' It's the same feeling I have right now. I'd lie on the floor of that swing and I'd feel it go back as hard as they could make it go, and my arms would straighten full length, fingers rigid, and my body would slide away from my hands, my legs sticking straight out behind me into the empty air, and then the swing would jerk and start back the other way." My voice cracked and I was almost afraid I was going to cry, but I went on. "And then my body would slide toward my hands till my fingers were still gripping, but now my stomach was over that end slat and I was hung over the awful air, my own weight pulling at me as if it were trying to kill me, until suddenly the swing would jerk back the other way."

Roman's hand cupped my neck. There was sadness and complete understanding in his eyes. "I could have gotten killed, Roman," I whispered. "I could have lost my grip and been thrown, shot out of that swing like a broken doll, and hit by the swing as it came back. And you know what? I couldn't stop doing it. I loved it. I was scared to death, and I couldn't stop. That's how it is now. This may be the worst thing that could happen to me. My father might not know me, might not want to know me, but I can't stop myself. I'm scared to death, but here I am, like I'm lying on the floor of this swing, yelling, 'Higher! Faster!' I'm scared, Roman."

"We can go back," he offered, but even as he said it, we both knew that wasn't the answer. I had come too far. No one had ever yelled "Stop!" in the middle of swinging. I didn't then and I wouldn't now.

I straightened and jammed my hands in my pockets. "No," I mumbled to him, to myself. "Let's go."

47 VanCouver. It was a gray brownstone, rundown and dreary, but in the window box at the top of the stairs were tremendous geraniums, a riot of red. We checked out the nameplates on the bells. 1—BRIGAD, 2—TAYLOR, 3—GERMANO.

"There's our man," Roman said, pointing to the first name.

"Are you sure?" I asked, that nagging part of me wanting to deny I was doing this, that this was possible. "It doesn't have his full name."

"It's just smudged," Roman told me. He faced me squarely, studied me. "Are you having a change of heart?"

Change of heart. What a strange expression. As if my heart were a kaleidoscope changing with the moment, with the tilt. No, I knew my heart was unchanging, like a locomotive hurtling down a hill. "No," I answered. "Just wanted to be sure I've got the right person."

I took a deep breath. I could feel the tension in my shoulders and the beginnings of a headache deep inside my eyes. I rang the doorbell, and Roman turned and walked down the steps.

"Where are you going?" I almost screamed at him.

He smiled. "To the door," he said simply. "The first floor is down here." He pointed to another stone staircase leading beneath the steps we were on, and I reluctantly followed him down.

"Are you sure, Roman?"

He didn't even answer me, just smiled.

We went down the steps and I could hear a rustling inside. A man's voice called out to us: "What? What is it?"

"Mr. Brigadier?" I asked. I could see an old man's face; he held a soft lace curtain aside and peered out at me. There were city bars on the window to this door and on the windows next to it, black wrought

iron that tried to disguise itself with innocent-look-
ing twists and swirls.

"Yes? What do you want?" I saw the man look
suspiciously over at Roman, who was on the step
above me.

"Hi. I'm Darcie McAllister. I tried calling you the
other day—"

The curtain dropped and the face disappeared.
I was stunned.

"Mr. Brigadier? Please!" I begged. "I have to talk
to you. I'm trying to find Paul Brigadier. It's very
important."

Roman put his hand on my shoulder, but I
shrugged it away and knocked on the door. "Please,
Mr. Brigadier. I won't keep you long. I just have
to know where I can find him. That's all."

There was silence.

"Oh no," I wailed. "Oh no. You can't do this! You
can't do this!"

"Come on, Darcie," Roman said, cupping his hand
around the back of my head. "Don't force it. Remember? It's not meant to be, that's all. Come on.
Let's go." He tugged at me gently, trying to ease
me away from the door. But I felt wild inside, lost.
I started pounding.

"Mr. Brigadier! Mr. Brigadier!"

Roman was nervous, trying more forcefully to
pull me from the door. "Come on, Darcie, stop.

You can't do this. He'll call the police. Come on. Come on."

A weakness came over me like sleep. I felt I was in a dream where all my strength was drained from me. My fists pounded softly, then not at all. But I couldn't leave. I sat on the bottom step, put my face on my knees, and cried. Loud and hard, like the small, abandoned child that I knew I was.

Roman ran up the stairs, looked around, and then came back down. He tried to lift me, but I wouldn't move. I couldn't stop crying. "Darcie, Darcie," he crooned. "Come on."

I would stay here. I would never leave. I would take root. Rot. This old man would have to climb out a back window to leave his apartment. I would turn to stone like a city gargoyle. And then I heard the bolt. A chain clinked. A knob turned. The door was open, and I looked up. A scrawny man in baggy pants and a thin, nearly transparent undershirt stood before me. He was looking down at me, something in his expression I couldn't read, and he leaned back against his door. He didn't say a word.

I wiped my wet face quickly with my hands. This wasn't at all how I thought it would be.

"Mr. Brigadier?" I whispered.

He didn't answer, just stood there.

"I'm trying to find Paul Brigadier. Can you tell me where he is?"

"Who are you?" he asked. "Denise McAllister's kid?"

I nodded.

"You don't look like her," he said. "Paul brought her around here a few times, a silly pretty girl, not like you at all. Funny how I remember my son's sweetheart better than I do my own." He sounded tired, worn.

"You're Paul's father?" I asked.

"Yeah," he answered, glancing at Roman. "Paul's father. That's me."

He acted as if he had suddenly had enough. He started to pull the door shut again. "Wait!" I said, jumping to my feet. "I need to know . . . about Paul. Where can I find him? Can you tell me? I have to find him." I could hear the panic in my voice.

Mr. Brigadier stopped and looked at me curiously. "Is George McAllister still around?" he asked. "Isn't he your uncle?"

"Yeah, he's around. I'm staying with him this summer."

"Well, why don't you ask him all these questions? He could tell you everything. I'm sure he'll tell you all you want to know."

I was suddenly struck with a feeling of hopelessness. I didn't think Uncle George would ever tell me anything. And now I knew, neither would this man, Paul's father, my grandfather. The door began to close, and then it stopped. The old man hesitated. I still couldn't read what was in his eyes until he reached out and ran a finger down the side of my face.

"Right around here," he said. "Along here. It's just like Paul. And your hair." Then I knew what it was—sadness, sadness and longing.

He closed the door and was gone.

"Oh, Darcie," Roman murmured. "I'm sorry," and when I looked up at him in the stairwell, light shone around him like an angel. He put an arm around my shoulder, and I followed him back up the stone steps.

I drifted in and out of sleep on the train ride home, as we sat side by side on the hard seats, rocking with the motion, the trains nearly empty now and heading back to where they had started.

"Darcie?"

I lifted my head and looked at Roman next to me. He seemed far away. His hands were clasped loosely between his knees and his whole torso rocked gently with the movement of the train. "Darcie, remember when you were talking about that swing? And how you'd think you were going to die, but you'd do it anyway, over and over?"

"Yes."

"You reminded me of something. Something I did long ago. When I was young, maybe ten or eleven, we lived by the railroad tracks. They ran right past my bedroom window out in the country. It was like this block of houses built along the tracks, and the rails were raised slightly on a hill that was overgrown with weeds and scrub oak and poison ivy." Roman didn't look at me, but straight ahead, and rambled on. "At first I used to put pennies on the track. Step over the third rail, real easy, center the penny just so, and then scramble down the hill and wait. A train would come by, screaming past, right up the hill where I could see underneath and watch the wheels flashing, and once it was past I'd look for the penny, and find it, flat and thin like paper."

His voice was faint and almost childlike. He sniffed and went on. "My mother found them in my pockets one day while my father was there. In the kitchen. 'Big deal'—that was his reaction when she showed them to him. 'Big deal,' he said. 'The kid's gonna get himself killed.'"

Two lines of tears ran down Roman's cheeks. "So I started putting other things on the tracks, toy metal cars, lead soldiers, keys, and then one day, I don't know, I guess it was the fear, like with that swing, the fear of the underside of the train, those wheels and gears and the noise. I started going up the hill at night myself and lying down on the ties, between the rails, in the darkness. I'd lie there and listen to the crickets, and the quiet, and then I'd feel it in the ground, the drumming, the rumbling vibration. It would get closer and closer, and there was always that moment when I could have run, could have rolled down the hill, but I never knew how long that moment would be, if I would make it in time, or if my father would find me like a flat lead soldier the next morning. I'd be scared, but I loved it. I'd want it, need that fear. I did it all summer long, lying on the tracks in the horrible noise, looking back at the shadows in the lit windows of my house, through the haze of steel wheels speeding by."

Roman turned and looked at me as if he'd been in a darkened movie theater and suddenly remembered I was there when the lights came on. I don't know what he saw when he looked at me. Maybe he saw my fear. For the briefest instant, I suddenly realized I didn't know who Roman was or where he came from, and just like the seals turning to sharks in the underwater shadows of the seal pond, something about Roman flickered before me like danger. Just for an instant. Then he smiled crookedly, once again the Roman I trusted, and he drew my head against his shoulder to rest.

But nothing was quite the same again. The chance of finding my father seemed bleaker than it ever

had, but I became single-minded and determined, maybe like someone drowning, right before
they go under for the last time. I wanted to find
my father, and if Uncle George was my only
link, I would find some way to make it all fit. But
like the child on that wooden swing, I was holding
on with all my strength, and I actually ached phys-
ically; my ribs hurt, my stomach, the sides of my
neck.

It wasn't till a few days later, late one night, that
I had a chance to find out more. I was lying in bed
sweating, the air heavy and still. It was late, but I
could hear someone stirring inside. I lay there listening. I listened for a cough or a sigh. I wanted
some ice water, but I wouldn't go out there if it was
Uncle George. Sometimes at night, in a drunken
fog, he would stumble around the rooms. But it was
quiet now. Nothing crashed or fell, just the silent
nighttime sounds of cabinet drawers, little clicks,
and a chair scraping.

I pulled my cotton nightgown over my head and
went into the hall. There wasn't much light in the
living room. It was dim, and in the darkness, I could
see wisps of cigarette smoke hovering over the room
at eye level, like a ghost. Someone had been sitting
there a long time.

Aunt May's back was to me, and my bare feet
didn't make a sound on the hall rug. A single over-

head light cast a circle around where she sat at the kitchen table; and a cigarette glowed in her hand. I shivered as I passed the electric fan. I pulled out a chair. It wasn't till I sat down across from her that I saw the album open on the table. She looked up at me and her face was slack. It was then that I noticed the wineglass at her elbow, filled with Uncle George's Scotch and an ice cube.

"So hot, honey, isn't it?" she asked.

"You okay, Aunt May?" I asked, reaching out to squeeze her hand and look into her drooping eyes.

"Oh yes, I'm fine," she crooned. "Just fine. It's just the heat. That's all." She took a drag on her cigarette, and as she did, a long gray ash broke off and fell onto the album page. She began brushing the ashes off, blowing on them.

"The album," I said. "You found it."

"Yes, I found it. I *hid* it. Thought better of the whole thing. I never should have let you see it in the first place. It was foolish. I should have put it away before you even came, but how was I to know you'd be so full of questions?" She began closing it, but I reached out my hand, trapping the page open, and pulled the book across the table toward me.

"I have a right to know, Aunt May, now that I want to," I told her. "Secrets never work." I looked down at the photographs. The album was open to pictures of their early marriage, Uncle George, dapper and smiling; Aunt May, pretty and young. I looked closely at a picture of them standing with a little girl between them, a little girl in a round, derby-type hat, who could have passed for their daughter, a corsage on her coat, and short white socks. The girl's hand was in Uncle George's. The camera had caught him with his glasses off, his eyes closed, and she was smiling. My mother.

"There are secrets about my father aren't there, Aunt May?" I asked, suddenly feeling angry at her for the first time. This was Uncle George's doing, but *she* knew. She had some answers, too. She had known all the while.

"No, there are no secrets," she said, brushing me off.

"I went down to VanCouver Street, Aunt May. I saw Paul Brigadier's father."

Aunt May looked up at me and her eyes blinked slowly, as if she were suddenly waking from a deep sleep. "What did he tell you?"

"That Uncle George could tell me all about it. Tell me about my father."

"Oh, Darcie," she sighed, shifting her weight away from me and grinding her cigarette to shreds in the ashtray. "Don't dredge this up with George."

"But *you* know what happened back then, don't you, Aunt May?"

"Yes." It was a word, a breath. She leaned back in her chair and waited.

But I didn't speak. I turned the pages, keeping time still, frozen in space like the photos. A life. This was Aunt May's life. The younger days, the husband, his little sister, the restaurant, the parties, the four-year gap, and suddenly pictures of the sister's young child, a little girl around three or four years old, in overalls and sneakers, unruly curls, grubby fingers, who would come and bring unspeakable hauntings with her. A little child who would never be told her own story, who would go through life never knowing—if everyone just kept quiet about it. And where in all this was Paul Brigadier, I wondered. What had Uncle George done? Aunt May brought the glass to her lips and drank deep and fast.

"Tell me, Aunt May," I said.

"Oh, it was a long time ago, Darcie. It was so long ago," she said. Her voice was flat and lifeless, like a recording. "He joined the army and went to Germany, I think it was."

"And what did Uncle George have to do with all this?"

"Darcie, Darcie. It's so long ago. I don't remember all the details. What difference does it make now? What good will any of this do?"

"Tell me," I demanded.

She tried to make it all sound unimportant, trivial. "George met with Paul before he shipped out. To settle any arrangements. I don't know what happened. I wasn't there. I just know Paul told your Uncle George that he was glad to be heading out and to be leaving all his mistakes behind him. Said he was off to make a new life."

"Did Uncle George tell my mother that?"

"Of course he did. He didn't want her pining away, waiting for Paul to come back and take care of her or something."

"How did Mom feel?"

"Feel?" Aunt May tucked some loose strands of her lifeless hair behind her ear and stared out the window. "She didn't feel anything. Well, it upset her at first, but she got over it. 'A new life.' That's what George told her Paul had said."

"Did you all believe Uncle George?"

"What do you mean? Of course—"

"But you saw Paul. You saw him yourself. Do you think he was really glad to just leave it all behind. Leave *me* behind? You knew he loved me. My mother doesn't even know that he saw me once, does she? She doesn't know how he felt about me."

"Yes, I told her eventually. Years later. She was glad he got to see you, Darcie, she really was, but she got over him. She knew it was for the best, eventually. They were too young."

"But she didn't know for sure how he felt about her, though, did she? You only have Uncle George's word."

Aunt May closed her eyes, "I don't know. I don't know," she said wearily. "It was so long ago. And it's always been easy to believe. Easy to put it to rest. Easy to have Paul out of our lives."

I felt as if I was going to throw up. My mouth tasted bitter. How could everyone just take Uncle George's word like that when it didn't make sense. Paul wouldn't have said that. He wouldn't have seen me as a mistake. I closed the album and stared into the spinning blades of the electric fan. "My mother never knew for sure how Paul felt, and now it's too late," I said, thinking of Ed and his woolen shirts, his brown leather jacket. Too late for her maybe, but not too late for me. "George knows that truth," I added.

"You're making too much of all this, Darcie. Don't talk to George about this. It will only make things worse. Really. It's not important anymore. It's better this way. This way your mother had a chance at a new life. She had a chance to grow up a little, you know? It was clean, it was quick, and it was over. Why should she have all that extra pain? All that uncertainty? Maybe if he'd come back. But he didn't. It never would have worked out."

I got up from the table. Without a word, I walked to my room. I must have looked like a dead person. I passed the door to Uncle George's room and I could hear him snoring, and even though I seemed dead on the outside, inside a flame of hatred and disgust flickered in me. I wasn't dead at all. I was a walking time bomb.

I didn't think much about Roman anymore.

I didn't care about the seals, either. The restaurant. Nothing. All I cared about was finding out what had happened to my father. And there wasn't much time left. I was putting in my last days, and soon the summer would be over. I didn't let myself cry or laugh or feel anything except this overwhelming determination to make some final sense of things.

Roman would whistle for me to feed the seals and I would ignore him. I guess I knew he would have told me to just leave well enough alone, so I avoided him. He would come by and knock on the counter, his smile now nothing more than a billboard expression, no longer touching me, stirring me. I told him I was busy. Told him I couldn't leave the cash register. And when he'd press me about it, laugh and try to ease me out of my mood, I would walk away from him.

I didn't care what jobs Uncle George told me to do, and as he ordered me around, I'd secretly question myself: Is this the right moment? Should I ask him now? It would have to be in the restaurant, while there were one or two others nearby, and before he began drinking.

This one afternoon Uncle George sent me away from the restaurant, almost as if he sensed a danger in having me around. He sent me out to the balloon stand for the day, because Venezuela had been picked up for running numbers again, the little illegal business he had on the side. I carried the cash box with me and a box of thick balloons. As I walked out of the restaurant and down the steps to the path, I felt how fleeting the summer had been, how soon it would be gone and I'd be back home, back in my own life. Venezuela would just be another South American country, and I would forget about the balloon stand, the zoo, Mary Dora, Roman, and the dream of ever finding out what had happened to my father. Unless I did something very soon. My summer days were washing away, just like the mulberry stains on my patio floor back home.

The balloon stand was still where Venezuela had set it up before he'd been taken downtown. There weren't many balloons left, so I began to blow them up one at a time, mindlessly looping them over the mouth of the helium tank, inflating, tying, and securing them to the hook on the side of the stand. Now and then a child would come by, or a couple, and I would sell them one and wait silently while they picked through the colors.

I was edgy. I went through the money box and turned all the bills green side up, right side around. I checked the dates on the coins, looking for one from the year I was born, but that stirred sadness in me like the beginnings of a toothache and I stopped.

I guess it was a beautiful day. The sky was brilliant blue, with clouds that looked unreal they were so white and soft. But I felt as if nothing could touch me. I followed the redbrick path with my eyes, remembering how I had loved the pattern and taken a kind of childlike pleasure in its magical vanishing point around the bend and into the zoo. Now, nothing.

The balloons tapped quietly against one another in the warm breeze above my head. I sat there all afternoon, until it was time to close. I had blown up too many balloons, and knowing Uncle George didn't like to store them in the back room, I decided to set them loose. I wound the strings around my fist and took them from the hook. They were knotted and I held the knot tightly in front of me, in both hands, and then, one finger at a time, I let go. The balloons drifted up, as if they had a life of their own, the whole batch of them. The knotted strings brushed through my fingers, and in a silent breath, a cloud of colorful balloons lifted into the sky, scattering, one or two wandering higher and farther than Roman could ever reach with his rescue balloon, higher than any ceiling of clouds and stars could hold. Gone.

Slowly and deliberately I locked up the money box, folded the stand, and rolled it all back to the restaurant.

7

Dear Darcie,

    Someday I will bring you to Israel. It captures my imagination, to walk these paths, to see plenty drawn from aridness, and to see faith grown from despair. I'm counting the days. I'm thinking of you as you were when you'd crawl up on my lap for snuggles. Are you really too big for that? I can't wait to see you again. I miss you terribly.

                          love, love,
                          Mom

The picture on the back of the card was an old painting of Daniel in the lions' den, a family of lean, wild-looking lions gazing up at Daniel lovingly as he stood before them, his arms raised in prayer, and two soldiers peering in the entranceway, their faces washed in disbelief. I had seen the picture somewhere before, maybe on the wall of an old Sunday-school classroom or in a child's Bible-stories book, and just seeing it gave me an unsettled feeling of timelessness, as if the past and the future were intertwined, mixed up, and I found myself vaguely *remembering* some future moment.

I slid my feet into the stiff legs of my jeans. My mother was counting the days. What did she think of so far away when she thought of me? What did she and Ed speak of when I came into the conversation? The passage of time and the flowing of miles had made me small to her, made me small enough to sit on her lap, and the same time and miles had made her youthful to me, a teenage girl with the hardness of my life growing inside her, beneath the elastic of her gym shorts and the pressure of her uncertain hands. I loved her, loved her, yet knew how little I really understood about her.

I pulled my jeans up, and folding the lions'-den card in half, I put it into my back pocket. I don't know why. Maybe out of habit. I wasn't thinking about Roman or about showing it to him. He wasn't on my mind at all. As a matter of fact, I was thinking about Ed. Thinking about how once, a while ago after dinner one night, all of a sudden, he had done an imitation of my mother. He had held his hands before him, glimpsed up to the ceiling with a half smile on his lips the way she does, and he had said, "Ed, all I know is, wherever I go, there I am," and I had laughed so suddenly, so unexpectedly, because he had done her, captured her on his own face so perfectly. It had made me uneasy the rest of the night, knowing how well he knew her, perhaps even better than I did.

I stared at my face now in the mirror above the dresser. I looked angry, my forehead creasing into a frown, my mouth turning down at the corners. I smoothed my hands over my face, lifted my eyebrows, my cheeks, my hair, willing myself to walk through another day. I didn't look back at my face, but buckled my belt, adjusted the pockets of my jeans, and straightened my T-shirt. Keep walking, I told myself. Keep going. This could be the day, the day I'd finally confront Uncle George.

I thought of being a child and waiting at the edge of a turning jump rope for just the right moment to jump in. The false starts, the body picking up the rhythm and imitating it before the wild dive to the center. That's how it was with Uncle George. I was waiting at the side, waiting for the right moment, waiting to jump in.

Uncle George was edgy when I was around. Any pretense at manners or tolerance had deteriorated into coldness and impatience between us. Everything I did annoyed him, and I eyed him with cold disgust.

At night I would count his trips to the cabinet to refill his glass, even from my room, where I could hear his heavy footsteps and the clatter of the ice cubes breaking into the sink. Once that began, I knew I wouldn't be able to speak to him at all. During the day, at the restaurant, I'd glance over at him to see if now was the time, and I'd see him suddenly look away. I was like a cougar in the bushes, stalking him, waiting to pounce, and he was my prey; he knew I was there.

How easy it all would have been had he been different. I could have sat down calmly and asked him about Paul. We could have talked about what had happened. But as the days passed, and the hours chimed repeatedly on the ancient clock above the restaurant, I felt less like a child waiting for the right moment to jump into a jump rope, and more like a souped-up car, getting psyched to fly through a flaming hoop as it sped past at blinding speed.

I misjudged. Miscalculated. It was out of my mouth before I knew what was happening. And it couldn't have been worse.

It was night and Uncle George was counting the money at the big table, shaking out the heavy canvas bags and sorting the money into loose piles. I blurted it out.

"Mr. Brigadier says you know what happened to my father."

Aunt May was there. At the sound of my voice she dropped a handful of loose coins and they rolled across the floor. Uncle George sat motionless and turned his face up to me. "Mr. Brigadier? Your father? What are you talking about, Darcie?"

"I went to see Mr. Brigadier over on VanCouver Street—my grandfather. I went to find Paul. But he wouldn't tell me anything. He told me you'd be able to answer all my questions."

Uncle George went back to counting his money. He seemed softer here, late in the day, before he'd had his drinks. I braced my arms across my chest and waited. I knew I was being crazy. Knew it and didn't care anymore.

"Ask your mother, for God's sake." He seemed fidgety and nervous, as he kept counting his money, licking his finger and flicking bills into separate piles.

"I'm asking you," I said.

"You don't want to hear it from me."

"Let me decide that. Where's my father? Where did he go?"

He paused, looked up at me and then down at the money on the table. He waved his hand over it. "See this?" he asked. "One night, I counted up four thousand of these nice green little ones, brought them over to your Paul Brigadier on VanCouver Street, and told him I thought my sister was too young to get married. I told him to join the army, or a circus, anything, and just leave Denise alone." He looked up at me and took his glasses off. His eyes were bloodshot. "And he bought the package.

That's what happened to your 'father.' Knocked up my sister and took a payoff to get lost. Worked out pretty well for him—"

"George, my God, how can you say that?" Aunt May stood at the other end of the table, but he didn't answer her.

"Did my mother know about the money?" I asked, my voice mostly air.

"No. All she knew was that loverboy took off, joined the army, and disappeared. It was like a toothache. All that pain and agony—one yank and it was over and done with. Thanks to mean old brother George." His hands were each clasped around a roll of bills.

"You robbed me of a father," I said, my voice coming from somewhere outside myself.

"Takes two, Darcie," he answered. "He took the money. He sold you to me for four thousand dollars, you and your mother. *I* could have been a father to you. May and I could have raised you, but your mother wouldn't hear of it . . ."

He lowered his eyes to the table, his lips slack, his words hanging in the air like bombs.

"You? A father?" I whispered.

"Or Denise could have stayed with us. But no, she had some crazy notion that Paul'd see the light one day and come back to her. She lived over a store all those years, even when she knew he was never coming back. Crazy kid."

I didn't know what I was doing. I took hold of the edges of the table to turn it over, to spill the money across the floor, but it was too heavy and I could lift it only an inch. I crashed it up and down that inch again and again, like a madwoman, my hair falling over my face, my teeth clenched together, coins spilling every which way. I screamed, "I hate you! I hate you! I could kill you!"

He bowed his head and sat there motionless.

I couldn't get my breath.

"You know," he said, "your mother used to worry that you never asked about your father, never wanted to know. I told her it was to your credit. That you knew to leave well enough alone." He looked at me. "It was better that way, Darcie."

My head was pounding. I didn't know what I was doing. It didn't matter. Nothing mattered. I ran blindly from the back room, out the screen door into the darkness. It was warm and damp and dark, and I was heading for the black void of the park, up the path, running from Uncle George, from the truth, from myself. But the back room of the birdhouse was lit. It glowed with the light of safety and escape. It was then that I thought of Roman.

He was sitting on a high stool at the worktable, and he turned when I crashed into the room, the door slamming against the wall behind me. We looked at each other and I remembered how I hadn't spoken to him all week, how I had pushed him away so many times, and how he'd been right all along. Seeing him there, I wondered how I had done that, stayed away so long, forgotten how I longed to be with him.

"Well," he said. Just "Well," and I waited in the doorway, my arms useless, my head still pounding with confusion, until he held out his arms to me and I went to him, was gathered in by him, and he held me close.

"Oh, Roman," I whispered into his collar. We held each other so close and so tight that my heart was like a balancing scale—sorrow and pain on one side, joy and pleasure on the other, so perfect, so equal, that I neither laughed nor cried but floated somewhere in between. Slowly, rhythmically, he rubbed the side of his face against my hair, and I closed my eyes.

In the next room, a large bird flapped its wings heavily, sounding like big sheets on a wash line in the wind. "Oh, Roman," I said again. It unlocked us, and he backed away from me and looked into my eyes.

"What is it, Darcie? What's happened?"

"It's been a terrible week." I looked cautiously into his eyes, remembering how I had ignored him all week, turned away from him every time he had reached out to me.

"I thought so," he said, wiping each of my cheeks

with dark fingers that smelled like apples.

We drew apart. I was uncomfortably aware of his thighs against mine, his chest, his hands. I couldn't think or speak with him so close. "It's about my father," I told him.

"Yes."

"After we came back from VanCouver, I asked Aunt May about it. She told me how Uncle George said my father ran away and joined the army. According to Uncle George, Paul was glad to get away, saying he was going to make a new start on life after getting my mother pregnant. But I couldn't believe that, Roman, I just couldn't believe it, and how could Aunt May? Not after she had seen how he was with me, when he saw me as a baby. He saw me once, you know. Aunt May arranged it when she was minding me one day. He loved me. I don't think he wanted to leave at all. He promised he'd come back for me."

I pulled up another stool and sat next to Roman, comfortably distant from him, but close enough that our knees touched. "But then, I don't know, after May told me about him taking off, and what Uncle George claimed he said, well, I knew I had to talk to Uncle George myself. I wanted the truth. I wanted him to say those things to me looking him right in the eye. I knew I'd be able to tell if he was lying. But I messed it all up. I was waiting for the right time, but I ended up just blurting it all out, about seeing Mr. Brigadier and all. And you know what he just told me he did?"

Roman shook his head.

"He paid my father four thousand dollars to leave."

Roman's lips disappeared beneath his mustache.

"I guess the worst part is, my father took it. Uncle George says my father sold me and my mother for four thou—" I started to cry. "Oh, Roman, you were right. I never should have searched for any of this. I can't believe it. It doesn't make any sense. I wish I never knew any of it."

Roman gave me a handful of tissues and waited as I wiped my eyes and my face and blew my nose. "Let's think a minute," he said. "Now that you know all this, maybe things aren't what they seem. Maybe George is just saying this. Trust your intuition if something tells you he's not telling the truth."

I searched his eyes. "You think so? Do you really think Uncle George might be lying?"

Roman shrugged. "Lying. Exaggerating. Not remembering it clearly. I don't know. But something in you is saying it's not right, that it can't be."

"Oh, Roman, if only that were so. If only I could believe that."

"Believe it. What have you got to lose?"

I stuffed the tissues in my back pocket, felt something there, and pulled it out. It was my mother's postcard and I held it in front of me, folding it and unfolding it.

"But, Roman, if I believe what Uncle George says, it's all over, the search, the hope, the belief that my father'd want to come back for me one day, even just to see me. But if I don't believe him, what's left for me to do? There's nowhere left to turn. There's no one left to talk to. Nothing."

"You could talk to your mother when she gets back," he said, and it was as if a black dropcloth collapsed over my head, smothering me.

"No," I answered sharply. "Not my mother."

Roman picked up an apple from the counter and began cutting pieces out of it. He fed us as he spoke, placing small wedges into my fingers or into his own mouth. "How about this Brigadier guy on Van-Couver again? What do you think he'd say if he found out that George paid his son to get lost, or do you think he already knows? Or maybe that's not his truth at all. Maybe he wouldn't buy George's story."

"He wouldn't see me again." I sighed, the apple wedge sweet and juicy in my mouth.

"You never know." Roman pressed another apple wedge into my hand and eased the postcard out. "Another card from your mother?"

I nodded.

"She's so nice how she writes to you all the time

from all over." I had to smile. I wondered what my mother would have thought of Roman. He's so nice the way he slices you apples, I could almost hear her say. He's so nice the way his shirt is open. So nice the way he looks at you. She wouldn't have said that.

He read the message and smiled. "Snuggles?" he asked. "Are you too big for snuggles?"

I blushed. I don't know why. I'm not sure if it was the thought of sitting in my mother's lap or his, but his smile teased and touched me in a way that made me restless and uncertain.

He turned the card over. "Daniel in the lions' den," he said thoughtfully. He looked at it for a long time. "That's so beautiful. What an incredible story. Can you imagine doing that?" His eyes were faraway, dreamy, as if he were about to recite poetry. "Testing like that, actually walking into a den of lions to prove that you're meant to live, that God's smiling on you?"

He looked back at me. The beginnings of an image ran through my thoughts—of Roman lying on the railroad tracks when he was a young boy. I pushed it away. I wanted to believe he had a special way of seeing the world, as if he weren't simply a person but something magical, deeper. In my mind I forced myself to see him covered with wildflowers, vines of blossoms growing from his pockets, berries in his hair, a bird on his shoulder, and gold dust sparkling off his fingers. He was like nobody I'd ever known in my life. "*I* can tell God's smiling on you," I said, and I reached out and placed my hand against the side of his face. He was warm, and his skin was rough and bristly to my touch.

We looked long into each other's eyes, and I felt his eyes were full of uncertainty, but it passed quickly and he smiled, pressing my hand to his face and kissing my wrist. He slipped my postcard into the front pocket of his shirt. "How about a walk?" he asked. "The park is wonderful at night."

"A walk? In the park? I didn't think it was safe."

"Oh, it's fine. For me. All the ghouls and the bogeymen know me. They don't mess with Roman Sandman."

"Are you sure, Roman?"

He slid from the stool and pulled me after him. "Leave your worries and your fears behind, raccoon eyes. There's a moon out there."

He led me out into the darkness of the zoo. Everything was so quiet and empty, like a haunted village, a ghost town. Just the small streetlights lit the path. I looked back at the restaurant; the Cadillac was gone. Uncle George had left me alone, taking Aunt May with him, and I took big steps to keep up with Roman as he turned down the dark path that led out of the zoo into the park. He held my hand in his.

It wasn't as dark as I had expected. The sky reflected the glow of the city. There were no stars, but Roman pointed to a crooked half-moon hung in the trees like a squashed paper lantern. The trees were black shadows and the moss-covered boulders rose around us like childhood monsters, but I wasn't afraid. Roman's step slowed and he was quiet. Happy. I could feel the happiness coming from him. And from me.

"Lots of lightning bugs out tonight," he said, snatching at the air and catching one. He stopped and held out his hand. In an instant the lightning bug lit like a street lamp, sending out a pale-green glow that illuminated his hand, and I saw the map of Roman's life in his palm, his life line, his love line, and I didn't know what any of it meant, but I felt comforted that it was so simple, his past and his future charted out in the cup of his hand for me to see and to touch. The lightning bug flew off, leaving the map and my finger touching there.

Roman led me off the path to sit beneath a tremendous old tree, a tree that reached far into the starless sky. We sat with our backs against its trunk, our knees up, our shoulders touching. We were quiet. All around us crickets were singing. There was even a frog croaking nearby, and off in the distance was the low swish of traffic like the sound ocean, and through the trees off to our right somewhere, red and green lights flashed on and off.

"I'd like to kiss you, Darcie," Roman said in the darkness.

I turned to look at him. He was in shadow, only the whites of his eyes and the white collar of his shirt were clear. I looked away. Uncertain, but not afraid.

"Yes, I would," he said. I turned to him again in the night, and his hand came up and cupped the side of my head, guiding me toward him.

I closed my eyes and gave my face to him. I felt his lips close over mine, his open, mine closed, his confident, mine timid. Slowly he pulled back from me, as if to look at me, and I opened my eyes. Close up, I could see his eyelashes. Feel his breath on my cheek. I closed my eyes and drew near to him on my own, this time my lips parted, and they met his, which were closed. We pulled away again, my eyes staying shut, memorizing the sensation as if I were drawing a picture of him, and he kissed me once more—this time his lips parted, mine closed. Some-where in the forest of my mind, beneath the warmth and the thrill, was the echo of knowing I wasn't doing this right. But he drew me close to him at last in an embrace, his cheek rough and loving against mine, and I could tell he was smiling. "I'll never forget that kiss, Darcie," he said. "Thank you."

I nestled in his arms and we leaned against the tree for a long time. Until we heard other frogs, different crickets, a siren, and even saw a few stars and a lone bat. "What will you do tonight?" he asked. "Your ride left."

"I don't know," I said.

"Want to stay in the birdhouse? I have a cot in the back room. It's not the most comfortable bed, but I've stayed there sometimes. It's not bad."

"Where will you be?" I asked.

"I'll go home."

"Is it scary? Alone in there at night? Aren't there vandals?"

"Nah. It's nothing to worry about. The back-room's never been broken into. If you want, we'll get Morgan, our old trusty vulture, to sit on the shelf over you and keep watch."

"No thanks. I think I'd rather deal with muggers and bogeymen than Morgan."

"And what will you do tomorrow?"

Things were beginning to come together in my head in the stillness of the night, in the safety of Roman's arms. I sat up and rubbed my face hard. "First thing, I'm going to go see Paul's father one last time," I said. "And that's it. I'll tell him what May and George told me, about the money and all, and then see if he knows where I can find my father. And if it doesn't work, if he doesn't know, or won't tell me, I'll let it go. I swear, Roman. I'll say, This isn't meant to be, Darcie, and I'll really let it go."

Roman stood up and rose above me in the night. I touched the hem of his pants and folded it in my fingers. He held out his hand to me and hoisted me up. "I can't go with you tomorrow," he said. "Okay? You'll have to do this one on your own."

I nodded. I had known that already. For some time I had had a real sense of how alone I really was. We headed back to the birdhouse and I thought of sleeping there. I hoped I wouldn't be too frightened. I hoped Aunt May wouldn't worry too much. Roman stopped suddenly on the path and pointed off into the bushes. I could see a bright, shining pinpoint of light, like a cigarette tip glowing in the dark, but no one was there. We stared at it and then went nearer to see what it was. Up close we found a spiderweb, a thin, laced veil of illusion, and hung from its center was a lightning bug, his light burning, not flashing off and on, but burning strong and bright like a beacon. Roman reached out gently with his finger to free him, but it fell to the ground.

At that moment I was overcome with such a feeling of dread. The lightning bug seemed like the last little glimmer of hope that was left to me. And was that all it was? Just the glow of a dead lightning bug with its light stuck on?

The thought of going on the subway was so frightening that before I even fell asleep that night, with my head cushioned on a burlap bag of soft birdseed, I was already planning how I'd get there on my bike. In the darkness I could see the shimmering lines of its spokes and I was comforted. My bike, that had helped me run away so many times, that had sped me away from my mother's sad eyes, away from things I didn't want to hear, tomorrow would take me to my answers, the very things I was ready now to hear.

When I woke up I could hear the rain battering against the green skylights above me, but there was no changing my mind now. I checked the city map that Roman kept tacked to a cabinet door and left for VanCouver Street before Roman even got to the zoo. I borrowed his black slicker, hanging on the back of the door. He would have to use a spare one to feed the seals or to go out, but that was okay. I wanted his. I wanted to feel him with me as I pedaled along in the pouring rain. I wanted to smell him all around me, as if I were in his skin.

The rain pelted me like angry hands as I rode along the wide avenues, weaving in and out of sluggish traffic. I watched the street signs, following the numbers down lower and lower until they changed to names, and then VanCouver.

VanCouver was shiny and slick, clean as a city street is clean at no other time. I found the house, locked my bike securely against a parking meter,

and went right down the stone stairs, not even ring-
ing the bell, but going straight to the door and
knocking. He was there. He looked out the window
in the door at me and opened it immediately.

"Mr. Brigadier?"

"I told you I had nothing—"

"Please wait. I spoke to my uncle like you said,
and he told me things. Things I'm not sure are true.
Things I can't believe about Paul . . . my father.
Please. Just let me see you a minute."

He hesitated. He looked at me, at my face, and
I held my breath, hoping that with my hair wet and
slapped down around my face I still looked like that
old memory of his son, enough that he'd let me in.
Talk to me. The door opened and I stepped inside.
He eased Roman's slicker off my shoulders and took
it into the bathroom, which opened off to my left.
I watched as he draped it on a hanger and hung it
on the shower rod. The bathroom was lined with
dull black tile, and there were towels hung over the
edge of the sink.

"Have a seat," he said, motioning to a table and
three chairs that stood in the center of the room.
Newspapers were piled high on one of the chairs.
I sat on an empty one, the one without the faded
corduroy cushion, and instantly a cat was on my
lap, purring and pushing her hips against my chest.
I patted her and waited while, without asking,

this man who I knew to be my grandfather prepared two cups of instant coffee. My grandfather.
I watched him, searched for signs of me in him but
saw none. Even his thumbs were straight as boards.
What kind of father had he been? What kind of
love had he given?

"No milk," he announced, placing the steaming
mug before me. It was stained with past coffees,
and I lifted it hesitantly to my lips, wanting its warmth,
yet uneasy, so uneasy. Part of me wanted to bolt
and forget the whole thing. He sat down in his chair,
the cushion conforming instantly to his bony shape.
He slurped the coffee loudly, lined up his spoon,
a pencil, a paper napkin, and then he looked up at
me. "Well? What is it you want, Darcie?" The way
he said my name, I knew he'd been thinking about
it, practicing it.

I stroked the cat from nose to tail, following the
run of her fur as she wound around in my lap to
sleep. I watched the silver-tipped hairs as they fat-
tened and puffed under my hand, and I struggled
to speak. "I never knew anything about my father
until just this summer . . . when I came to stay with
my aunt and uncle. They have a photo album. I
saw pictures." I looked up at him wondering if he
had ever seen those pictures. "Then there was so
much I wanted to know. My aunt told me how my
father came to see me once when I was a little baby.

He had held me. He promised to come back."

He nodded without any expression on his face, so I went on. "Then she tells me that he just took off, joined the army, and he told Uncle George he was glad to leave and start a new life. Glad to start fresh without past mistakes. As if he were glad to leave my mother and me behind."

He had stopped nodding. I thought maybe he had stopped breathing, he was so still. "When I saw you, you said George had all the answers, and I tried to talk to him." I remembered the night before and squirmed uncomfortably in my seat. "He's not easy to talk to, you know." My grandfather bit the side of his lip.

"He told me that my father took money to get lost and leave my mother. That he sold me and my mother for four thousand dollars."

I held my grandfather's eyes in mine, two straight, watery eyes, heavy like paperweights in his head. "I don't want to believe that," I whispered. "Tell me he's a liar."

"He's a bastard," he answered in a hoarse voice. "A bastard."

"Did my father take that money?"

The old man rose and walked to the counter. The cat jumped off my lap and went to him, rubbing against his legs, mewing and thrashing her tail. He ignored her. "George McAllister came by here one Sunday morning. He left a large envelope on the table. He told my son that he was too young to take over the responsibility of a wife and a child, and that he wouldn't give him a nickel's worth of help if he insisted on marrying her. But he told Paul if he joined the army, and stayed away for two years, that when Paul was discharged, if he and Denise still wanted to be together, he would do all he could for them. He'd even give Paul a job at the restaurant." My grandfather looked back at me. "Apparently that's not what he told Denise, though. Denise McAllister." He shook his head as if to clear it. "I hadn't heard that name spoken out loud in years. Not until you came. Standing there with Paul's face just as clear as a neon light on you."

I lowered my head, ashamed of my face, sorry that it hurt him.

"But Paul never kept that money," he told me. "He gave it back."

"He did?"

"Yeah. That same day. After George left and Paul opened it and saw what it was, he took it over to the restaurant and gave it to George's wife . . . what was her name?"

"May?" I whispered. "May?"

"May! That was it! He told her he'd join the service and stay away for two years, but when he came back he was coming back for Denise and his kid, and he wouldn't need any job at the zoo, either." He snorted and looked at me. His eyes had suddenly turned red and his voice cracked. "And of course, he never came back."

But I wasn't listening. I felt as if I were shrinking, like Alice in Wonderland, growing smaller and smaller as I sat on that chair in that basement apartment on VanCouver. The room grew immense around me, and my heartbeat was nothing more than a cricket's, dry and silent. Aunt May? Aunt May had kept the money and never said anything to my mother, to Uncle George, to me? She had known everything, the whole story, and had never let my mother know? How had it been that morning? I pictured Paul handing the envelope over to Aunt May, refusing to be paid off, refusing to sell me. What had they said to each other? Full, hot tears poured down my cheeks. Hadn't Alice flooded a room with her tears and floated out a keyhole?

I stood up before it was too late. The cat passed between my feet, leaning hard on my legs. All this while I had thought Uncle George was the villain and Aunt May the innocent victim. I wanted to go home. To my own room, my own kitchen, and I wanted my mother there. I wanted the familiar nearness of her, the comfort.

I stumbled to the door. I didn't want to hear any

more. I didn't want to look at this sad old man
another minute. There were chains and bolts on
the door and I fumbled with them madly, locking,
unlocking, the door not budging as I pulled it and
shook it.

"You are impatient like your father," the old man
said. He handed me Roman's slicker and reached
past me, turning the locks in succession, slowly, me-
thodically.

"I don't want to hear it," I shouted. "I'm sorry,
but I just don't want to hear it."

I burst out into the pouring rain. It ran down
my arms as I thrust them into the sleeves and then
fumbled with my bicycle lock. My hair was hanging
in wet strings against my neck. The bike seat was a
puddle. I had to see Aunt May. I had to let her
know what I knew. That she was as bad as Uncle
George. Worse. I'd let her know.

The rain had eased to a drizzle by the time I
biked back to the park. And I watched Aunt May
walking toward me for a long while before I realized
who it was. She was just a gray form in the gray
day, her raincoat gripped closed before her, her
head bent against the drizzle. She must have been
at the administration building. I got off my bike by
a bench, dug the kickstand into the mud, and waited,
watching her approach. She didn't look left or right,

just down at the ground ahead of her, and it wasn't until she was right in front of me that she looked up and gasped.

"Darcie! Where have you been? I've been sick with worry! You can't do this!" She was starting to raise her voice. "Your mother would be furious if she knew what was going on."

"Would she be furious to know about the money, Aunt May?" I asked.

She had no idea what I was talking about. "What money?"

"Four thousand dollars."

Her face had all the expression of a park statue.

"The four thousand dollars that Paul gave back to you. Uncle George never got it back, did he? He doesn't even know that Paul didn't keep it."

"Oh, Darcie. Oh, Darcie," she said, and her bottom lip began to tremble. "What have you done?"

I stared off into the distance, not even wanting to look at her. "I went to see my grandfather again."

Aunt May stumbled over to the wet bench at the side of the path and sat down. She buried her face in her hands. "Oh, Darcie," she said again.

"Stop saying that!" I shouted.

She began to cry, but my heart was like concrete. I felt nothing for her. "What did he tell you?" she asked.

"The whole thing," I said. "I know everything

you did. Everything except what you did with the money, and I'm sure that's not important now."

"I *bought* you things," she said, staring down at her hands. "Remember the red-and-white-check coat I bought you that Christmas?"

I wouldn't answer.

"And your first two-wheeler?"

It had been powder blue, with a big basket and silver streamers coming out of the handlebars.

"And the ring for graduation from grammar school?"

I had lost it already. I began to remember how Mom and I had this little joke about Aunt May, how she would send gifts and things I needed and always tell Mom not to tell Uncle George. We'd joke about how Aunt May must have had something going on the side to make extra money. We even thought maybe she helped Venezuela out with his numbers. Now I knew.

"Why'd you do it?" I asked, looking at her.

"I didn't want George to know, because it would have upset him. I didn't want him to know how determined Paul was to come back. I just wanted him to think he was getting his way. I tried to keep things as calm as I could, for as long as I could, you know? I didn't want George upset. I've always done that. Sometimes it's been like standing in the ocean and trying to calm the waves with the palms of my hands." She held out her arms before her. Her hands were trembling. "I did it for him," she said simply, turning to look at me. "I did it for George."

I sat down on the bench and looked at her. She was pathetic somehow. All my anger drained away, leaving me empty and weak inside. "Oh, Aunt May," I sighed. "Why'd it have to be this way?"

"I don't know," she answered. "And then, when Paul was killed, none of it seemed important anymore, you know?"

I turned to meet her eyes. "Killed?" There was a silence roaring in my ears. The rain, the traffic, the trees, the animals were all still. There was only the sound of that awful, final word. "Killed?" I asked again.

Her voice was small and shallow. "I thought you said Pete told you everything."

I stared at her. "Not this," I whispered. What had he said? I tried to remember. I pictured him standing there at his counter, a small man, stooped, dusty-looking. He had said Paul told Aunt May he'd join the service but he'd be coming back for us. And then he said Paul had never come back.

Aunt May leaned back on the bench and sighed. Her coat opened, but she didn't seem to notice. The fabric of her dress grew dark with the fine mist of rain. "It was a barracks fire, or something in Germany. Wasn't even a war. Just some careless fire or explosion, they said it was, and Paul was right there. They said he died immediately. It was terrible."

A shudder went through me. Thinking about my father dead was like a screw being turned deeper and deeper into the hardwood of my heart. The deeper it went, the more I knew it was true, as if I'd known all along, and the tighter it wound, the more violent I felt. George McAllister had robbed me of a father. Hadn't he killed Paul Brigadier just as surely as if he had set the explosions under him himself?

Aunt May looked over at me, but I didn't move.

"You could've put a stop to all this, Aunt May," I said. "Anywhere down the line you could have taken a stand."

"No, Darcie. I couldn't. I couldn't do anything other than what I did." She stood and looked at me for a minute. When she spoke, her voice was hard and unfeeling. "Come back to the apartment to-night. Don't stay out again." And she walked away, back down the path to the zoo, to the restaurant, to George.

I waited until she was out of sight. I snapped and unsnapped the clasps on Roman's slicker, waiting. I was wet inside and out. When she was gone, I mounted my bike and slowly and deliberately followed where she had led. Most of the outdoor cages were empty, the crowds were gone, the balloon stands were closed up, the seals were in their caves.

I rode to the restaurant, the gears on my bike delicately clicking along the service path, and around to the back door, where the Cadillac stood. Summer thunder rumbled far away, maybe in New Jersey, I thought, as I leaned by bike against a tree and took my key out of my jeans pocket. I grasped the key in my hand, pressing my curved thumb along the length of it, and with a steady pressure I walked around the Cadillac, digging the point of the key into its luminous paint. Along the doors, back door, front door, the fender, the hood, the other fender, the other doors, the back fender, the trunk. I walked around it three times, thinking how the high screech sounded awfully like a small monkey with its foot caught in a trap.

8

When I was little Aunt May would bounce me on the crook of her ankle and sing, "East Side, West Side, all around the town." I abandoned my bike behind the restaurant, and a little haunting voice sang that to me as I roamed around the city on foot. Only now I was no longer a small child; I was grown, a woman, and I clutched Roman's slicker to me as I wandered from the East Side to the West Side, through strange neighborhoods where the blocks, and even the languages, were unfamiliar to me.

I kept my head down, and when my feet ached from my wet sneakers rubbing on raw skin, I would rest in coffee shops, having cups of sweet tea and tearing paper napkins into confetti for the silent waitresses to clean up. There was nowhere to go. My mother wouldn't be home for another week. I couldn't go back to the apartment. I was homeless and cold, even though it was warm and muggy out. I had been wet for so long in the rubber slicker that I was chilled to my bones, and every once in a while I would tremble uncontrollably.

I must have walked for hours, and I could have walked more, but it was growing dark and I began to feel frightened. It wasn't a conscious decision, but soon I found myself at the gates of the zoo, the only place that seemed even faintly like home. Maybe I could spend the night in the birdhouse again. I thought of Roman and my step quickened.

As a child I had once gone to sleep with rubber bands wrapped around my fingers, only to wake in the darkness with my fingers throbbing and pounding, swollen like balloons. Then, as now, I had run for help, bursting into my mother's room, to her bed, bringing my pain for her to ease. Her hands had trembled as she carefully dug the points of scissors into my fingers, snipping at the rubber bands and freeing the circulation of blood. I had screamed with pain, the blood rushing in like fire. Even now, as I ran to Roman, I could once again feel the fire in my fingers. What had I done? What awful thing had I done that changed my life like this?

I was praying that Roman had stayed late. That he might be sleeping himself on the cot where I had slept the night before. I was running now, through puddles, over the wet grass, following the green, glowing street lamps along the path to the birdhouse. I could feel that he was in the zoo. Somewhere nearby. Why hadn't I thought of him sooner? Roman. Roman. He was all I could think of. He would know what to say.

The birdhouse was lit, but Roman wasn't there. I called out to him, in the back room and then in the large bird room. There was a fluttering, a squawk, but no Roman. I paced outside at the door, frantic now, in the dark, in the silence, and I began to hear a sound. It was a moaning, or a crying, and the hair stood up on the back of my neck. Without thinking, I wandered away from the birdhouse, toward the sound, toward the seal pool, rigid with horror, but my feet taking me forward.

There was a figure splashing in the water at the edge of the pool, and all the phantoms in all the lagoons I had ever seen came back to me. It was dragging something, trying to lift something out of the water. It was a man crying, and then, "Oh, Ray," he wept, "oh, Ray."

"Roman?" I whispered.

The man froze. It *was* Roman. I could see his hair now and the shape of his shoulders against the lamplight. "Who's there?" he shouted.

"It's me. Darcie," I called, and I ran to the railing. "What's happened, Roman?"

He sobbed and pushed his hair back with his hands. I could see he was all wet, and at his feet at the edge of the pool was a wire trash can. Somehow, trapped inside, nose first, the lower half of his body free and limp, was Ray Charles, wet, black as a starless night, and motionless. "Help me, Darcie," he said weakly. "Maybe he's still alive."

I was over the railing and at Roman's side in an instant. I threw off the bulky black slicker and worked with Roman to free Ray's flippers from the broken wire, to keep his nose out of the water. He was the heaviest thing I had ever felt, but Roman worked frantically, straining and sobbing, until at last the basket pulled off and Ray Charles was like a born baby, slithering into the water. A born dead baby. Dragging and pulling, floating him through the water, we got him to a slab of rock. I don't know where we got the strength, but we hoisted him up, rolling him out of the water, and Roman immediately jumped up beside him and tried to revive him, pushing on his barrel lungs, lifting his flippers as if they were arms. Water poured from Ray's whiskered lips, the lips I had kissed almost every day all summer. His eyes were closed. I knew he was dead before Roman would believe it. I held my hand on Ray's head, the water rushing over my legs, and like a child does, I tried to pray him back. Just let him live, bring him back and I'll do anything. But Roman sat back on his haunches at last, buried his face in his hands, and cried.

I sat there motionless, staring into the darkened trees. Words floated into my thoughts, comforting words about death. What was it my mother had said to Ed that afternoon, when Ed cried about his brother's death? They escaped me, like minnows in a pond, brushing the back of my hand but gone, so close but gone. I couldn't remember, and I sat there useless. Silent.

Finally, crying myself, and not knowing what else to do, I crept to where Roman was and put my arms around him, holding him tight and feeling his ribs heave inside my grasp. "Oh, Roman," I whispered. "It's so sad, Roman."

What a sorrowful fountain we would have made there on the rocks in the center of that seal pool— some forgotten myth about a man and a woman and a sleeping seal, and water could have shot up out of our embrace, or cascaded behind us down the higher boulders. Part of me wishes that we could have turned to stone there, like a fairy tale, exactly like that, in each other's arms, and somebody would have made up a story to go with it. A story about the seal keeper and the girl who would even kiss seals for him.

Roman's sobs calmed and he seemed to relax in my arms, his cheek hot on mine. "How can I stay on here without Ray?" he whispered. "I can't live without him."

I put my hands on his head, my fingers weaving into his wet curls. "You'll stay, Roman," I told him. "You'll get over this." But even as I said that, I wasn't sure I believed it. Would I get over what I had just learned? Would *I* ever laugh again? I pulled his head back to see into his eyes, to make sure he was there. But he was glassy-eyed, and his face was swollen. I wanted to tell him about my father, but decided not to. Not yet.

His arms, which had been around me, dropped to his sides, and he sank to the ground. "Maybe I'm not supposed to go on, you know?" He looked up at me, and then around at the darkness that circled us like a gaping mouth. "I don't understand this phantom Death. How do we know he's not coming for us? Right now as we sit here?"

All around me sharks shimmered beneath the cool black water.

"I'm gonna test Death tonight," Roman said. There was a sudden strength to his voice, an unexpected determination, and he stood up over Ray's dead body. "Yes, let's see if Death is coming for *me* to-night."

Roman leaped from the boulder into the water

and waded to the railing. He turned back and looked at me, my creature from the lagoon. The water glistened black around him—sharks and monsters, phantoms. "Will you come?" he called.

I went toward him, wading through the black water with my heart in my throat, imagining black blood swirling around my legs, calling out to the sharks. I went toward him. What else was left for me to do?

I followed Roman back to the birdhouse, and when I went inside, he was pulling sheets and blankets off the cot. He was rolling them over his arms. "What are you doing?' I asked thinly.

"You remember that card your mother sent you?" he asked.

I touched my back pocket. Where had it gone? "Where she asked if I was too old to snuggle?"

Roman pulled the card out of his own front shirt pocket. It was soggy, but he unfolded it and gazed at it. "Daniel in the lions' den," he said simply. "This is where I'm going. To test Death. To have Death and God fight for me tonight."

I didn't understand, and I wanted desperately for him to make sense. "Roman, don't talk like that. You know you're meant to live. You're full of life. You're more alive than anyone I know."

"Then come," he said, looking up at me now and holding out his hand, palm up. "Come with me if you think I'm meant to live. You'll be my lucky charm, my madstone."

I didn't move.

"Where else have you got to go, Darcie? Who else wants you tonight but me?"

His eyes held me. I felt myself wavering. My father was dead, my mother was gone. Aunt May and Uncle George had betrayed me before I was even born. He was right. No one else wanted me tonight. Roman did. His wet clothes clung to his muscular chest and his arms that I loved, and his hand, scarred and tanned, so tender, reached out to me. His eyes, oh, his eyes, pulled me in, and I was like a fish on a hook, and the hook had swallowed deep, latching on to my soul, and I found myself moving toward him, my hand out, my eyes wide open.

"*You* believe in me, raccoon eyes. You'll make it happen."

I can't explain it, or describe it, just as I can't describe a color with words, or a bird call with hand motions, but I knew then—just as I had known that bright summer morning, when he had asked me to kiss Ray Charles for the first time—that there wasn't anything I wouldn't do for Roman.

I held Roman's hand as he led the way through the zoo, running silently along the paths and through the grass. I felt great danger all around me. The animals no longer seemed like gentle creatures locked inside safe cages, but like wild monsters unleashed, stalking, waiting to devour us. The hyenas cried in the distance, and somewhere a giant cat screamed. A halo of fog encircled each of the street lamps, and suddenly two headlights lit the path from a distance. Roman ducked behind a cluster of bushes and we stayed hidden while Murphy cruised past in a patrol car. Crouched down in the bushes, still wet and chilled, Roman drew close to me and whispered, "An imaginary menagerie manager imagined he managed an imaginary menagerie."

I stared at him in the faint light. The sadness had left his face, but I wasn't sure what had replaced it. He seemed determined, relaxed, now that he was settled on some purpose. His mustache and lips formed a smile, but not his eyes. I stared back at him.

"Can you say that three times fast?" he asked.

"Stop it, Roman," I whispered.

When the patrol car was out of sight, Roman stood up cautiously and began running again. He led me to the House of Lions. Outside, the cages were empty, swept clean, and a tree with large seed-pods rattled by the bars, warning me, I thought, but I didn't listen, drawing closer to Roman, holding his one hand with two of mine. We went inside the building. Roman had a key. It was dark inside but for the pale city night sky leaking down through the green skylights and the red exit signs over the doors. It was an eerie, beautiful light, reminding me of the painting of Daniel in the lions' den, Daniel with his arms raised.

Our footsteps echoed. All around us were the sounds of breathing, snoring, and low, growling stretches.

Roman handed me the bundled blankets and tried the keys to a back room. Key after key failed to unlock the door, and then suddenly it opened wide into an office and supply room. A light had been left on on the desk, casting a golden glow on everything about me. Roman approached the desk and put the postcard there on the blotter. He smoothed it out, examined it carefully, and then took the position Daniel held in the painting, the position I had thought of only seconds before. He reached his hands up as if in prayer and leaned back slightly, his back arched high and his face held up. I felt I was living in an unreal world, where I could sense the future or create an image merely by thinking of it. I clutched the blankets tightly.

Then Roman turned to me and held out his arms. This was enough. It was all I really wanted or needed, and I hoped he would feel it and it would be enough for him, too. "Tell me I'm meant to go on living, Darcie."

"You are, Roman, I believe in you." I pressed my face to his shoulder and let the blankets drop to the floor and my arms encircle him. "What would the seal pool be without you? And how would they ever get Ike out of the restaurant? And how about Rebecca? She'd never get to smoke."

Roman chuckled and held me tighter. "You're right," he said, and then, "Are you ready?"

"For what?" My voice as small as a hummingbird's. My heart rattled like the seedpods.

"To test Death," he answered, and he lifted the blankets and took me to the hallway that led to the cages. I followed, like a trusting, blindfolded child follows a friend through the house, with every sense and awareness raw like a wound. I followed him down the hall and he stopped before a metal doorway. He put a small key in an opening, pushed a button, and the metal door slid up with a loud hum. He ducked inside, drawing me in with him, and then, once through the door, he put the key in another hole and the door hummed shut.

It was dark, just the green-red glow of skylights and exits. I was inside the lions' cage, and instantly I had an image of standing on a church altar, looking down at the pews, seeing things from a new direction. I pressed myself against the metal door, barely breathing, and looked around the cage. Off to the right was a whole country of golden fur, hills and valleys, still tails and heavy paws. I knew there to be five lions, huddled together in sleep. One lioness lazily lifted her head and looked at me. Her eyes closed and her head collapsed back on her sister's haunch. We were in. They were sleeping. I could get this close to Death, closer than any swing had ever swung me, closer than any railroad track had ever taken Roman. This close.

Roman was in the opposite corner, spreading the blankets out. "Darcie," he whispered. "Come here. Stay close to me."

Pressing along the wall, I crept to where he was. I didn't want to breathe or make a sound. He sat on the blankets and motioned for me to sit by him. I wanted to stand, to be on my feet, but I did what he said, never taking my eyes off the lions. Roman was more relaxed, almost too calm. My jeans were damp and stiff on my legs. Both of us were soggy from the seal pool, but we settled down close to each other, and Roman drew the blanket over our legs. He put his arm around me. "There," he said, like a mother.

He became very still beside me. And we sat silently for a long time. Then I realized he was crying. I tucked my hand under his leg. "Shhh," I whispered, frightened that he'd wake the lions. "It's okay. It's okay."

"I can't believe Ray Charles is gone," he said. "I

just can't believe it." He sobbed loudly, but the lions didn't stir at all, so I began to talk to him, to try to comfort him.

"He was very old, though, wasn't he, Roman? He couldn't have lived much longer."

"But what an awful death," he said through clenched teeth. "How could anyone have done such a thing? Killed an old seal?"

"It wasn't on purpose, do you think? Maybe some kid threw that old basket in there and Ray just got curious about it."

"It was a murder," he answered, not listening to me.

"Sometimes there are accidents," I said, as something began to clear in my own head. "Actions set in motion by different forces, and then things happen. No one means for anybody to die. Everyone wants what they want, but not for somebody to die."

"You don't know," he said, looking out the bars, away from me.

"I do, Roman. My father is dead."

He turned back to me. "Oh, Darcie." His arm tightened around me and he touched his forehead to mine. I think he expected me to cry, but I didn't. It wasn't the time to cry now. My thoughts were clear.

"Uncle George *did* pay him to join the service, and promised him a job in the restaurant after a while if he and my mother still loved each other. But Paul gave the money back to Aunt May before he went away. He really wanted to come back for me and Mom one day. And then he died in Germany. In an accident. I've been thinking Uncle George and Aunt May had killed him, you know? Because I was so close to it. But they didn't. They didn't mean for him to die. It was just a bad mistake."

"You mean your father has been dead all this while?" Roman asked.

I nodded. "Since I was a baby. I guess my mother had always been trying to tell me."

"Then he's always been with you, Darcie."

"What do you mean?"

"Well, he hasn't been staying away from you, or in another country, or raising another family. He's always been right here with you."

I felt comforted, as if a warm blanket had just been tucked in around me. "And Ray Charles," I told him. "Now Ray Charles is always with you, Roman, because you loved him." I sat up, completely forgetting the lions. "Wait a minute. It's coming to me now!" What my mother had said to Ed that afternoon. What was it? What was it? About love and death . . .

"I got it!" I cried. I knelt up before Roman took his two hands in mine. " 'Set me like a seal,' " I told him. " 'Set me like a seal upon your heart, for love is as strong as death.' "

Roman laughed. " 'A seal upon my heart'!" He threw back his head and laughed the rich laugh I had heard so many times before. " 'A seal upon my heart'! Oh, Darcie, you are wonderful. And where did you learn that?"

"A Cryptaquote puzzle," I lied, and behind me a lion yawned loudly, ending in a deep growl, and I remembered suddenly where I was and huddled next to Roman.

Close there beside him, circled with danger, protected by fate or luck, Roman seemed like an island of safety, and I grew bold inside. I glanced at him in the green-red light and he turned to me. I looked away and then back again.

"Roman," I began, but I had trouble going on.

"What is it?" he asked.

"I love you," I said.

I pressed my fingers to his lips when he began to speak. At least this time he didn't pull away from me.

"I know you think saying I love you is like putting bars around someone—" I looked around us and had to smile at the irony of where we were, what I was saying, and then I froze. "Roman," I whispered, with a sudden new wisdom. "You've put bars around me. You must love me, too."

He studied me a moment and then slowly un-
wrapped himself from me and the blankets. He
stood up with his arms lifted in prayer. I glanced
nervously at the lions. "Roman!' I gasped.

"Yes, Darcie. I love you," he said loudly.

"Please!" I begged him. "Sit down here."

Roman sat back down beside me and pulled the
blankets tightly around us again. Outside, the zoo
clock chimed once, and a lilting refrain of Old
MacDonald rolled over the restaurant, over the hills,
and through all the sleeping cages of the zoo.

I dozed off and on, short fitful spells of sleep
that were filled with dreams and images, none of
which I could remember, but each one left me with
a taste of terror in my mouth. We slept close to each
other, with our hands intertwined. At one point I
could no longer sleep. The skylights were beginning
to glow and the birds had begun to twitter outside.
I held Roman's hand in both of mine and looked
at it. The back of it was tanned dark, with little
white scars here and there along his fingers. I touched
each smooth scar. His knuckles were rough and I
smoothed them. His thumb curved slightly back,
but not as much as mine. I turned his hand over
and ran my finger along his palm to his wrist. There
across his inner wrist, almost like two bracelets, were
two white scars that seemed to glow in the dim light.

I felt him wake up, and his fingers curled over mine and held me.

"What's this from?" I asked, touching the scars on his wrist.

"A meeting with Death," he answered.

"What do you mean?"

He ran his own thumb along the scar, from one end to the other. "A knife that I've used to amputate diseased claws, or to repair wounded beaks—I cut deep and smooth, and it burned like fire, but it was easy. Skin is soft."

I stared at him blankly. "You mean you cut your own wrist?"

"Once in the autumn. I get so sad in the autumn. And when that didn't work, again in the winter. When it wouldn't snow."

"But, Roman, you could have died!"

He smiled, "Yes. I thought of that. I just never thought I could have lived, too. Death keeps losing with me. I don't know why."

He didn't know why. I thought of Uncle George saying Roman was crazy. He had warned me to stay away from him. I looked around me now. I was sitting in a lion's cage with five lions who would soon wake hungry and irritated. I felt sharks and bats and spiders, and Roman's hand in mine no longer felt loving but like that of a dying animal who wouldn't let me go. It was that awful gravel-up-my-nose feeling, at the point where blood begins to drop onto my open palm. Only now there was no one to run to.

"Roman," I whispered, getting up on my knees, watching the lions and frantically trying to gather the blankets. "Let's get out of here!"

"No, Darcie. Wait."

"Roman, I said let's get out of here now! Have you ever seen these cats when they wake up? They're hungry! And they're mean!"

"That's the test," he said. "Let's see if we're meant to leave this cage like Daniel did. It's not so impossible. It's been done."

I stared at him. "That's a Bible story!" I whispered. He wouldn't get up from the blanket, and I tossed my half in his lap. "You're not trying to prove you're meant to live! You're trying to prove you're supposed to die, aren't you? Aren't you!"

I had to get out of here. "Give me the key, Roman, and come on." I held out my hand. Maybe my father died young, never knowing much of anything, never seeing me again, never experiencing all those things we could have done, but I could still go on, go on with my life, and at least live longer than he had. I was all that was left of Paul Brigadier. I was a Brigadier myself, and I knew I was not going to be breakfast for five lions.

"This is *your* lions' den, Roman, not mine. The key!" I wonder if he would have given it to me if the door to the House of Lions hadn't opened at that moment and if the entire building hadn't flooded with light. At the same instant a couple of the lions lifted their heads. Would they begin to think of breakfast now? The old lion stood, stretched, and then began a slow walk around the cage. Slowly, heavily, his feet fell silently on the cement floor, while the footsteps of a person echoed down the center of the large stone room. I didn't take my eyes off the lion, but I held my hand out for the key before Roman's face. I watched the old lion's deep golden fur, his full mane, his black nose, which he wet lazily with his tongue. He began circling the cage like a weary old king, as if he was done sleeping and now it was time for something else. He approached the wall where we were and stopped. I was rigid with terror and shrank against the wall. All I could think of was the sight of the lions tearing meat so easily, with giant teeth and claws. He held me in his gaze. Would he know I was harmless? Or did I just look like bones and meat, warm and fresh from the hunt?

While he stood there looking at me, I heard the man's footsteps approach the cage and he came into view. The lion turned to look at him. It was the lion keeper, the man I had seen so long ago, on that first morning. "Keeper," I said evenly, desperately. "Keeper!"

He stopped and stared up into the cage. "Jesus

. . . Mary . . . and Joseph . . . What are you doing?"
There was such a look of horror on his face that if
I hadn't realized the full impact of what it was I
was doing, I knew now. I knew by his face, like a
face in a news clipping. Like a mother watching a
house burn with her children inside.

Roman knelt up beside me. "Don't worry, Murray. God will send an angel. Death won't touch
us."

"Get us out," I pleaded. "Please, get us out."

But the man just stood there. "Roman Sandman.
What in God's name—"

"Now!" I shouted.

The man held his hands up to quiet me. "Don't
move!" he said. He was trembling, as gray as the
stone at his feet. "Just don't move an inch! Got that?
I've got to get help." He ran from view and I could
hear him in the office where we had been, and I
could hear him talking on the phone in a panicked
voice, shouting, saying, "Hurry! Hurry!"

I wanted to cry, but I was too frightened. I thought,
I may never cry again. And it was all that I wanted,
the luxury to cry, to wail. But I just sat there frozen
beside Roman. The old lion had moved on for now
and returned to the other lions. But he sat there
awake, waiting. Roman took my hand as if to comfort me, but I pulled it away, wrapping my arms
around myself.

Murray was back outside the cage like a man standing on a high-tension wire. Over his shoulder was a fire extinguisher, and he held the hose in his hand. "Listen," he said, trying to sound calm. "There's a team coming right over that will get you out. Have you got the key to the cage opening there, Roman?"

"Yes," he answered resignedly. "It's here." He held the key out and jingled it.

"Damn it! Don't move! Just sit there. We don't want to open that door yet, because it makes the same noise as the entrance to the outside cage, and it might just trigger their hunger, you hear?"

I nodded, my teeth chattering.

So we waited—Murray rigidly on guard in front of us with his extingisher, Roman with his head on his knees, and me using every bit of my strength not to scream and go banging on the opening to the cage. I knew Murray was right. I knew he was right, and I just kept repeating that to myself over and over.

Soon we heard the zoo truck pull up in front and the sound of running footsteps. They were shouting, calling orders, but as they burst into the House of Lions, a hush fell over them and they ran to where Murray was standing, five or six men with more equipment, power hoses, and one had a case, which he opened hastily, and drew out a rifle. There were three rifles, and he plugged each with darts. Another vehicle pulled up outside, an ambulance, I guessed, by the lights that flashed across the ceiling like red bats.

"Are you okay?" one of the men asked. His face was kind and he was looking at me. He seemed to be the leader and I nodded. I could hear Murray saying something about Roman being the seal keeper and I was the McAllisters' kid. "Good, then listen to me. We want to get you over to the door where you came in, you hear?"

Roman lifted his head. "You've ruined everything," he said in a flat voice.

"Roman, listen," I hissed at him.

"They're not supposed to be here," he said to me. His eyes were so blank. Oh, where did my laughing Roman go? "They've ruined it all."

"No, Roman," I murmured, remembering my love for him and reaching for the last bit of feeling I had. I leaned close to him, whispered in his ear. "They're angels," I told him.

He looked at me and then out at the men. "Angels?"

"Yes! Now listen."

The man continued. "We're going to hold the lions off if we have to. And you're going to ease your way—very slowly—over to that door. The minute you get there, unlock it very carefully, and

Murray will help you out. But remember, just don't buzz that door open till you're ready to get out and get out fast, because those lions hear that sound this time of the morning and they think Meat. Got it?"

"Yes," Roman answered.

"Give the kid the key," the man ordered. "Let her go first."

Roman dropped the key into my open palm.

"And wrap those blankets around your arms, like this." He pretended he was winding them around his own arm and held it up before him like a shield. "And use it to protect yourself if you have to."

Roman and I wound the blankets around our arms with as little movement as possible. I thought of those big teeth sinking into my arm, my leg.

"Okay, now as slowly and as quietly as you can, I want you to start for the door. Got the key ready, honey?"

"Yes," I answered, clutching the warm key in my sweating hand. The lions were all awake now, and watching us and the group of men that stood at the foot of the cage. I looked at the men. They all stood ready, aiming at the pack of lions with hoses and rifles, and behind them four men in white, with stretchers and medicine bags ran silently past into the office.

I got up from my sitting position to my knees as easily as I could. And then to my feet. My thighs felt weak and aching. Roman was moving beside me, but I wasn't watching him now. I kept my eye on that door, that gray metal door that waited for me, that slowly drew closer and closer. A lioness got up and walked toward us.

I felt a small wail grow in my throat, but the leader of the men was saying, "It's okay, it's okay, she's just checking you out. She's curious. We won't open up unless she gets mean, so just let her look. That's all she's doing. Just let her look all she wants. That's it. There you go."

I wouldn't look at the lioness, but I felt her there. My arm beneath the rolled blanket throbbed. I was sure I could feel her breath on my legs. Another lioness got up and joined her. I started to cry, but I kept moving toward the door and got there first, before Roman.

"Now, when you're both there," the leader said, "just put the key in the lock and turn it. Just remember, the second it's open, *move*."

I checked that Roman was behind me. He was right there. Our eyes held for the smallest instant, eyes that had nothing left to say to each other. Turning, I saw three lions standing before us. I could have reached out and touched each of them. But I reached out with the key to the lock, grasping it in both my trembling hands. It fit smoothly into the lock and I turned it. While before everything

had moved so slowly, as if under water, now everything went too fast. The metal door slid up with a
loud hum. There were sudden growls and snarls,
and an arm reached out and pulled me through
the opening. I was carried along the corridor to the
piercing sound of horrible screams and shouts, men
yelling, "Get them back! Watch it! Watch it! Now!
Now! Now!" I heard the metal door hum shut again.
The screaming stopped, but not the growls. Or the
shouting or the roaring sound of water, or the rifle
shots. Roman wasn't with me. Someone sat me on
a stretcher and laid a hand on my head. Then the
floor came up and smashed me in the face.

I think it's late morning. The light is beginning
to change in my room as it does every autumn, the
earth tilting even more toward winter, threatening,
unstoppable, but now I've surrendered to it. I even
look forward to the leaves falling, the cold sneaking
into my coat along my collar and my cuffs. I've
already taken out my old leather cowboy boots that
I love so much. Mom says they're ragged, but they're
so familiar to me, like my own feet. It's all right.

I can hear Ed outside mowing the lawn, probably
for the last time this season. I know it's him and
not a neighbor, because I can hear him singing. He
has a terrible voice and knows it, so the only time
he ever sings is when something noisy is happening,

like showers, vacuum cleaners, or lawn mowers. He doesn't realize he can still be heard, and like a flying fish suddenly appearing out of the ocean and skimming across its surface, I can hear his voice above it, and I like him.

I should get up soon. But it's nice lying here this way in my own bed, with my own things around me. I have a nice black gooseneck lamp on my night table, my books, and the framed picture of my mother and my father at the sweet-sixteen party. Mom bought me the frame, a beautiful wooden one.

And we finally talked. When I came home I didn't want to run away anymore. Actually, at first, I didn't even want to leave her side, and we talked almost constantly. About Paul and what it had been like for her. About Uncle George and Aunt May and the money. Mom hadn't known about the money, but it didn't make her angry, just sad. She loves Ed now, I know that, and I guess she sees her life as working out all right, but she understands how it is for me, how I'm sad not to have my own father. That's why she gave me this frame, I guess, and showed me the other pictures, old movie stubs, and the pressed lilacs.

In the beginning it was really hard for me to tell her about Roman. At first we just looked at the newspaper clipping together and said nothing. "Terrible accident and human tragedy," they say.

"Roman Sandman, well liked by his colleagues here . . . Miss McAllister, who was questioned by the police in the hospital yesterday, was unavailable for comment."

And then slowly I began to tell her about Roman. I remember how she laughed when I told her about him smoking with Rebecca. I told her how he loved Ray Charles, and about all those summer afternoons of flinging dead fish through the clear warm air. The mosaics in the subway. The mad drummer. She just listened. And then after a while we put all the clippings in a big envelope along with all her postcards, all but the last one, which was lost, and the telegram that I had never seen until they got home that Monday. I put the envelope on my closet shelf, high up, almost as high as those old subway mosaics.

But, you know, I still think of Roman once in a while, the way he was, or the way I *thought* he was. And who's to say that wasn't a real part of him? He'd once told me that he meditated every morning. He had called it "lifting his heart and stepping back from his life." I try it, but it's hard. I guess I find it a little easier to step back from my life than I do to lift my heart.

My heart. Maybe it's hard to lift my heart because of the tiny seal I imagine to be tattooed there.

I should get up. But once again I lie here with

my eyes closed, making my world as dark as a cave. I close my eyes and turn my face toward the corner of my room. In my mind, I see wall meeting wall, ceiling meeting corner, and there, leaning against the pink flowered wallpaper—as clear as ice—I can see Roman. As he was. I see him tall and tense, his blue jeans faded pale blue across his knees, his green work shirt open over his throat and bare chest, and he's eating sunflower seeds, tossing his head back and shaking the cellophane bag over his mouth.

He says he's waiting for me. But I know I'm not coming.